ABSOLUTELY CHALKED OFF!

The Further School Diaries of Morris Simpson, M.A.

ABSOLUTELY CHALKED OFF!

The Further School Diaries of Morris Simpson, M.A.

JOHN MITCHELL

Foreword by Jack McLean

Drawings by Weef

Hodder & Stoughton
Published in association with
TIMES SCOTTISH EDUCATION SUPPLEMENT

Also available by John Mitchell:

Chalked Off! The School Diaries of Morris Simpson, M.A.
0 340 54363 9

British Library Cataloguing in Publication Data
Mitchell, John
  Absolutely chalked off!
  I Title
  823.914 [F]
ISBN 0 340 56188 2

First published 1991

Typeset by Rowland Phototypesetting Ltd,
Bury St Edmunds, Suffolk
Printed in Great Britain for the educational publishing division of
Hodder & Stoughton Ltd, Mill Road, Dunton Green. Sevenoaks,
Kent by Clays Ltd, St Ives plc.

The characters and situations in this book are entirely imaginary and bear no relation to any real person or actual happening. Cross my heart and hope to die . . .

John Mitchell
July 1991

Acknowledgements

Thanks, again, to all of the teachers whose stories have found a way into this book, whether they meant them to or not.

Again, special thanks to Jim Dunbar – a particularly efficient mole – as well as to my sisters and to Judith, for other tales out of school.

Thanks also to Willis Pickard, WEEF, all at TSES, and to Jack McLean. At Hodder, particular thanks to Brian Steven and everyone else who helped prepare it, and also to all who sold this one and the last one – especially Iain MacGregor and Jim Cowan!

Again, a mention for the girls: to Alyson – for eventually going to sleep at night and letting me think up another bit; to Kathryn – for sneaking upstairs now and again for a cuddle and then helping me to print out another bit; and to Judith – for sometimes letting me off bathing the first two so that I could finish *writing* another bit!

Finally, thanks to mum and dad for everything, not least for teaching me to read in the first place. This one's dedicated to them.

Foreword

In Germany the dominie is called 'Herr Doktor'. In France he – or she – is known as 'professeur'. In Italy 'Professori'. In Scotland a teacher is succinctly described. In Scotland a teacher is called a balloon – at least he is if he resembles the hero of this book, Mr Morris Simpson. Morris is, in short, a prat, a jube-jube, an idjit. A teacher. He is now of course an experienced, sort of, teacher. Seven years in the business. But Morris is more than that. Morris Simpson is now a Scottish institution. There are those who suggest he should be *in* one and in a straitjacket to boot. But Morris is still around, ready and willing to destroy the last vestiges of an educational system once thought of as the best in the world.

And what a world ago that was. Back in the days when Scottish education was the envy of . . . why am I going on like this? Scottish education hasn't been the envy of anything other than social work departments in years. Morris Simpson would make a rather splendid social worker, possibly a head of a Regional department. Morris is incapable of learning from his appalling experiences. Until now.

Morris has learned enough from his last two books to represent himself now as nearly sensible. What is beginning to concern myself, as a thankfully ex-teacher, is how his author, Mr John Mitchell, can continue to live with Morris, let alone bring him to life. For Morris is a nightmare. But then, so is school.

Discover in this volume how much of an incubus these places are. Discover how Morris almost gets promoted. Discover how you would be well advised to send your children up chimneys for an education rather than to an institute of learning. And if you are a teacher yourself, discover how your reality is much like that of every other teacher.

Mr Mitchell has an unerring eye and ear for the absurdities of Scottish educational life, more's the pity. He has become the chronicler of Scotch schools. He makes you laugh and greet. He makes you think, which is a damned sight more than educationists have contrived to do over the last three decades. Mr Mitchell, in other words, is my candidate for Secretary of State for Education. The reality is otherwise. John Mitchell will continue to delight in his history of Morris Simpson. Morris Simpson – or someone very like him – will doubtless end up in charge of the whole shebang. And serve us right at that.

Jack McLean,
The Glasgow Herald

Prologue: August 14th

'No man in his right *mind*,' emphasised David Pickup sharply, 'would ever *dream* of becoming a teacher!'

It was a claim which Morris Simpson had heard before from Pickup's lips. Often. He bowed his head slightly as Pickup ordered another pint for each of them and began to elaborate upon his theme:

'What a bloody job! Every day it's the same! Where else would you put up with it, Morris? Disobedience, aggression and sheer bloody rudeness – and that's just from the other members of staff! My God! When I look at some of the piles of mince that turn up as *pupils* in my classroom, it makes me want to weep! Talk about the future of the nation! God help us all if our prosperity's dependent upon . . .'

Morris Simpson (assistant English teacher at Parkland Community High School) let his attention wander. He was used to

1

receiving the embittered advice of his middle-aged colleague. He was also used to ignoring it. David Pickup (nothing-point-five geography teacher, nothing-point-five assistant principal teacher of religious education at the same school) had been a kindly enough mentor in Morris's early teaching career; indeed, Morris still enjoyed the friendly atmosphere of their more-than-occasional visits to Parkland's local hostelry, The Pig and Whistle. But he had recognised in the early days of his teaching career – five long years ago now – that Pickup's particular brand of cynicism would never lead to the early promotion he so earnestly desired.

'Oh, come on, Pickup!' he chided his colleague: 'it's not as bad as all that.'

'Isn't it?' spat back Pickup, glad that his young protegé was at least willing to join battle. 'Can you *honestly* say that you're looking forward to going back next week? Can you? And with Rose McShane's young brother about to join your first year registration class?'

Morris shuddered. It was true that the departure of Rose McShane from his teaching timetable during the previous session had been a cause for major relief and celebration. And it was equally true that, during an integration day with Parkland High's feeder primary school some six weeks previous, an incident with Rose's brother Tommy had led to a major breach of school discipline which had resulted in the eventual flooding of the junior boys' toilets. But the memory of his subsequent conversation with the McShane sibling had faded over the summer break. It had probably been an isolated incident, he tried to reassure himself – and Pickup.

'Oh, I don't think there'll be any trouble with young McShane,' he enthused confidently. 'I had very strong words with him last June, and he looked pretty crestfallen afterwards if I remember rightly. Told him he'd have to change his tune now that he was coming to a *secondary* school –'

Mr Pickup cast a doubtful frown, but Morris brooked no contradiction. 'And anyway,' he continued happily, 'nobody could *ever* make my life as much of a misery as big Rose McShane –'

'Hah!' interrupted Pickup. 'Don't you believe it, Simpson. For every Rose McShane that gladdens a teacher's heart by leaving school at the end of their natural span, there's always some other twisted little bastard springing up at the other end of the queue. And I'd say that if that little swine's got blood-ties to Rosie McShane, then there's more than an odds-on chance that he'll be as gormless, as obstructive and as argumentative as his big sister ever was!'

'Look, I'm sorry, Pickup,' Morris refused to be goaded any further. 'I know you don't like children, I know you don't think much of the job, and I know you've spent the best part of five years trying to persuade me to leave it. But I'm not going to!' His voice raised slightly in pitch. 'And anyway,' he continued in further self-justification, 'I think this could be my year for promotion.'

Pickup's eyes raised themselves heavenwards. 'For God's sake, Morris: you never give up, do you?'

'What d'you mean by that?' snapped Morris.

'Nothing, nothing,' apologised Pickup quickly, unwilling to be drawn into a detailed discussion of Morris Simpson's promotion prospects. In his eyes, they were less than zero. But he knew that Morris lusted after nothing so strongly as his first step upon the ladder of educational advancement. Pickup fully recognised, of course, that the incompetence which Simpson displayed in the normal course of his professional duties would be no real barrier to such advancement. Indeed, in many cases of which he had personal knowledge, such a grand level of incompetence would appear to have been a positive *recommendation* for promotion, for he had lost count of the number of glowing testimonials he knew head teachers to have written in order to rid themselves of particularly troublesome members of staff. However, it had become abundantly clear to him that, in the case of Morris Simpson, not even John Ross could bring himself to recommend the lad for a promoted post, no matter how dearly he would have loved to see the back of him.

For once overcome with tact, however, Pickup kept his thoughts to himself, and decided to change the subject.

'Another drink, old son?'

'Must we?' Morris dug a reluctant hand into his pocket. His parents would wonder where he was, and it was already near to closing time.

'Of course we must,' Pickup slapped his young friend on the back. 'And what better toast than the forthcoming term?' he suggested, as yet another round of drinks found itself a place on the bar.

'Oh, all right,' slurred Morris, by now ever so slightly the worse for wear. Arm aloft, he signalled an over-exuberant salutation to 'The New Term!'

'And all who sail in her!' laughed Pickup with him, as they clashed both glasses with just enough force to send their respective contents awash to the floor beneath.

'Oh dear!' sniggered Simpson. 'Naughty naughty, Mr Pickup!' A boyish laugh, then two imperious commands: 'Punishment exercise for you, sir! And a cloth please, bartender!'

An onlooker frowned across the bar. 'Bloody teachers!' he muttered . . .

It is always difficult to avoid gatherings of teachers in public houses. They will usually be loud, because that is the nature of their job. They will usually be complaining about their conditions of employment, because they feel that nobody else works as hard as they do. And they will always be discussing their pupils.

Morris Simpson and David Pickup were no exception. But Morris Simpson, it has to be admitted, was an unusual case. Some five years previous, he had been plucked from obscurity (an obscurity, indeed, which his professional competence probably deserved) by a chance encounter with a newspaper representative. Here, at the start of his teaching career, he had been offered the unprecedented opportunity to record the daily round and common task which befell the modern teacher at the commencement of his professional life. The newspaper in question, the *Times Scottish Education Supplement*, had seen fit to provide regular payment for the journalistic meanderings which Simpson, in his turn, saw fit to provide under the encompassing columnar heading of *Probationer's Diary*.

It was a column which was intended to last for two years, the normal probationary span of a virgin teacher in Scottish education. The fact that Morris Simpson was unable to become 'a fully certified teacher' (as he himself so unfortunately put it) until after his third year of teaching was not entirely his own fault. Suffice to say that the column (later retitled 'Morris Simpson's School Diary') continued unto its third year and beyond.

As did the books. It was a source of some professional pride to Morris Simpson that his diaries began to be issued in a more permanent form than that which is normally accorded to newspapers. Firstly, of course, there was *Class Struggle: A Probationer's Diary*. At the time of writing, this first volume of the Simpson educational memoirs remains unavailable, though Simpson himself has been besieged by requests (four letters to date) for the tome's reissue. Of more immediate commercial success was the publication of *Chalked Off! The School Diaries of Morris Simpson M.A.*, a text which became an invaluable resource for researchers wishing to record the practicalities of teaching life in a typical comprehensive school of the late 1980s. And now, in the 1990s, Morris Simpson is pleased once more to accede to demands for this, the publication of his third volume of educational memoirs.

Simpson has admitted, in all honesty, that he has been nonplussed by the commercial success of his school diaries. He has been even more surprised, we understand, to discover that his texts are more often to be located in the 'Humour' section of Parkland Bookshop than upon the shelves devoted to the more complex matters of educational theory. It was always his earnest hope that the diaries would serve to assist emergent teachers in their search for educational truths, and he has frequently requested a category shift for his books from the manageress of the shop in question. To date, she has proved unwilling to comply.

Such reservations about marketing policies notwithstanding, with the publication of *Absolutely Chalked Off!*, Morris Simpson looks forward to an enhanced reputation in educational circles.

It is, we venture to suggest, a pious hope.

The New Session

Those readers who have already met Morris Simpson will know him to be something of an amiable – if likeable – incompetent. In the more precise Scottish vernacular, he has been frequently – and, alas, accurately – described as 'a bloody great tube'.

Who else among the staff of Parkland Community High School was actually looking *forward* to the coming term? Who else would have dismissed the imminent addition of Tommy McShane to his register so lightly? Who else would actually *volunteer* to be staff representative on the new school board? And who else would report to school two days before it was absolutely necessary to do so?

It is with such ambivalent – and perhaps judgemental – thoughts in mind that we turn, once more, to the continuing school diaries of Morris Simpson. It is August. For most members of staff, the term

7

is due to start on Wednesday. For pupils it will start on Thursday. But for Morris Simpson, keen as ever, it began on Monday.

Monday

Last two days of the summer holidays. Eager to prepare for the challenges of the coming term, I nipped into school this morning to pick up the English class lists from Simon Young, my temporary principal teacher.

I was surprised to discover the place deserted except for two of the office staff, neither of whom seemed able or willing to help me. It appears that Simon hasn't been seen within the environs of Parkland High since the last day of June, and isn't expected back until first thing on Wednesday morning. He hasn't even been in to check up on the spring examination results.

'Well, what about Mr Parker?' I enquired of our recently appointed APT (assistant principal teacher) guidance, and in overall charge of my first year registration class. 'Has he left my class list for 1P?'

'Shouldn't think so,' scoffed Mrs Thomson. 'Haven't seen *him* since June 28th at the sixth year end-of-term party. He 'phoned in sick the next day and only managed to stagger along on the Friday to report himself in attendance to Mr Tod in case he lost his holiday pay. Then he went home.'

'But hasn't he got anything ready for the new first year? I want to get a list of my registration class so that I can start learning their names. How can I do that if I don't have a list?'

'Search me,' offered Mrs Thomson. 'Try coming in tomorrow. The headmaster might be around if you're lucky.'

It's hardly very impressive when promoted members of staff can't even be bothered to come in for some pre-season preparation. What do they *do* to earn their extra money, I wonder?

Tuesday

Popped into school again this afternoon, but only the headmaster was in evidence, hurriedly dashing off a note to the regional offices about our programme for tomorrow's in-service day. They had wanted to know why he hadn't yet sent a detailed account of the day's planned activities, in accordance with their request of last May.

Mrs Thomson informed me that Mr Ross had consequently spent a frantic morning assembling a collection of videos and instructional

8

manuals for Standard grade assessment, with which he planned to enthral the staff tomorrow.

I decided not to bother him about my class lists and went home to work out some lesson plans instead.

Wednesday

First day of term. Despite bitter experience, I entered the school gates this morning with a tangible feeling of optimism for the session ahead. In particular, I was looking forward to tomorrow, and the chance of instilling the first year with a pride in their new school, and a determination to work well and play well in their future academic careers.

Sadly, it seems unlikely that they will have much of an example to follow in some of their teachers: Mr Parker eventually turned up twenty minutes after the day had started, while Mr Pickup spent the best part of the morning complaining bitterly about the 'ridiculous waste of time occasioned by these ruddy in-service days'. And perhaps he had a point.

Mr Ross's presentations were uninspiring, to say the least. He spent some fifty minutes reading through every divisional circular which had arrived on his desk during the summer recess, after which he padded out another half hour by drawing our collective attention to the fact that – for the fifth year running – a new heating element had been installed in the staffroom tea urn, and that staff were henceforth forbidden, absolutely, to leave it switched on all day.

'Apart from the cost to the region of replacing elements,' he criticised angrily, 'they've also had to fork out for a complete replacement of all the wallpaper that's peeled off because of the endless steam belching out. It's not good enough,' he berated a practically comatose audience: '– and if something isn't done about it, it's almost certain that my request for a second staffroom pool table will be turned down by the divisional education officer.'

Suddenly, the whole room was alert. Frank Parker glanced nervously at Major, who nudged Mr Jackson soundly in the ribs.

'Jacko,' he whispered hoarsely. 'Go and switch the damned thing off, will you?'

As Mr Jackson scurried away to the staffroom, Mr Ross nodded triumphantly before calling a halt to the morning's proceedings. To a chorus of muted groans, he announced details of the afternoon's programme.

*   *   *

'It's a bloody disgrace,' swore Mr Pickup over a lunchtime pint of lager, 'having to justify every blessed minute of the day with a structured programme of in-service provision, when tradition has it that the day before the brats arrive is reserved solely for cleaning out your cupboards and making up your registers.'

I refrained from mentioning my failed attempts to compile such a register last Monday, as Mrs Convery chimed in:

'Hear! Hear! And it's worse for us in learning support,' she bleated plaintively. 'Not only do we miss out on getting the class lists compiled, but we don't even have time to write the kids' names on their jotters for them.'

'You *what*?' I burst in. 'You don't mean to say that you write –'

'Of course,' she arched an impatient frown across the bar. 'They can't do it themselves, can they.'

'Oh, come on?' I queried in disbelief. 'I know that kids today are only semi-literate, but talk about molycoddling them! How will they ever *learn* to read and write properly if their highly trained teacher spends valuable time writing out their names on their jotters for them?'

'Oh shut up, Simpson,' burst in Frank Parker. 'At least I can guarantee you one thing: it's a damned sight more useful way to spend your time than whatever the boss has got dreamed up for this afternoon.'

And so, alas, it proved. In addition to a tiresome spiel on whole-school policies relating to continuous assessment, we had to sit through a sleep-inducing document on administrative procedures for Standard grade. As far as I was concerned, the only spot of interest came from the headmaster's account of our proposed school board, to be set up this term in accordance with Government guidelines. This is an area of school life in which I intend to display a keen interest. Mr Ross explained that we would need two staff representa-

tives, and that he would be looking for volunteers quite soon. I had my hand up for quite a long time in an effort to attract his attention, but he appeared not to notice me. I shall see him privately as soon as possible.

Thursday

Tried to see the headmaster about volunteering for the school board this morning, but he asked me to leave it for another day. I must say, I thought he might have been pleased to get such an early response from a member of staff. In point of fact, he looked positively discouraging, but I didn't have time to follow it up because my first year registration pupils were waiting for their introductory talk.

I was somewhat distressed to discover that the only record of their names in my possession was a barely legible, scrawled list on the back of an old jotter which Frank Parker had pressed upon me at five past nine this morning. It was with some amusement that most of them greeted my consequently garbled attempts to read their names out loud when arranging their seating, and their shouted comments of hilarious correction rather spoiled my intentions to start off with a serious pep-talk.

A greater source of distress, however, was the discovery that Tommy McShane is a member of 1P. This odious little boy, whose path I first crossed at the end of last session during a primary integration day, looks set to follow in the ill-disciplined footsteps of his elder sister Rose, whose attendance and behaviour records would have been better suited to the girls of St Trinians than to Parkland High School.

Even so, it came as some surprise when, at the end of the first period, the young McShane presented me with a disciplinary record card for my signature.

'But this is only your first day, Tommy,' I confronted him. 'How can you be on one of these already?' I brandished the card aloft.

'Dunno, surr,' he complained. 'It's no ferr. Ah didny dae nuthin'.'

Faced with such a comprehensive denial of guilt, I decided to make no further enquiry and ticked the box marked 'Average' for each section of behaviour and attainment. It wasn't until later that I heard about the nails in the staff car park . . .

Friday

A fierce argument with Frank Parker this morning, which I lost. The problem arose at registration when Graham Taylor, a belligerent little boy from 1P, presented me with a letter from his mother, the import of which (as he told me before I could open it) was that he was 'gaun furr a hoalyday next week'. The letter confirmed it:

Dear Sir:
Graham and I and his father are off for haveing an extra holliday in Scarburou for the next 3 weeks, so Graham will not be at the school.
And oblidge
Michelle G Taylor (mrs)

And that was it. No request, no apology: simply a reporting of the fact that this child was to miss three of the most important weeks in his school career. I saw red.

'Maybe *you* think you're going on holiday, young man, but I'm not so sure. As your register teacher, I would have to sanction this unofficial absence, and I'm not sure that –'

'Aye, ah um gaun', surr. Yoo canny stoap me. An' anyways, yoo're no' ma Guidey: Mr Parker is, an' he seys ah kin go awright.'

Silenced by such bare-faced arrogance, I sent him back to his place and took it up with Parker, his guidance teacher, at morning break.

'The boy's quite right, Morris,' he informed me. He *is* going to Scarborough, and there's nothing you can do to keep him here.'

'But surely as his register teacher, I can –'

'Look, Morris, you could be his ruddy probation officer for all I care. If the boy's parents are taking him on holiday then there's nothing we can do to stop them, even if he is missing out on his first three weeks of school.

'Oh, and don't forget,' he added in afterthought as he walked away: 'you'll have to prepare a scheme of work for him with assessment items and homework built in. His mother asked specially for that: she was anxious in case he missed anything important while he was away.'

I glowered at the irony, but held my tongue.

Meanwhile, the headmaster continues to avoid my offer of assistance with the school board. His response at lunchtime was that there had been 'um, a great deal of, er, interest from, um, other staff', and that he might need to hold a ballot. It was news to me that anyone else was interested, but I thanked him for the information and hurried off to take 1P's first English lesson.

The class took some little time to settle down: they were understandably excited at the end of their first week, and news of Tommy McShane's immediate two-week suspension for spitting at Mr Major had caused a degree of exuberance as well. I must admit that it was difficult to maintain order, especially when confronted with Graham Taylor's smirking little grins of superiority. I decided to rise above the whole issue and not mention it again; instead, I handed him a jotter with three weeks of hastily constructed homework, and told him to enjoy his holiday.

My heart sank as he brought the jotter out at the end of the period. 'Surr?' he asked. 'Ye've no' written' ma name oan ma joattur.'

To my horror, a queue of fourteen pupils had formed behind him, all with the selfsame request, to have their names inscribed on their jotters for them.

Hand clasped to my forehead, I gritted my teeth and started to write. I get the feeling it's going to be a long term.

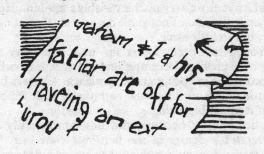

September

Morris seemed to have drawn the short straw when it came to the allocation of first year classes, for 1P did appear to have more than its fair share of under-achievers, with all of the attendant disciplinary problems which such a class would invariably cause him. He brought the matter up with Simon Young at a departmental meeting early in September, but to little avail.

Simon Young had been 'acting up' as a temporary principal teacher since the previous December and – after nine months in post with no word of his job being made permanent – he was beginning to lose a little of the organisational enthusiasm with which he had approached it in the beginning.

'No can do, Morris,' he responded unsympathetically to Simpson's request for a change in the first year class lists. 'Luck of the draw, really. Let me know if they get too stroppy and I'll nail them to the wall. Otherwise,' he continued maliciously, 'you'll just have to depend on your charismatic personality to carry you through.' And, with an ill-concealed snigger, he drew the meeting to a peremptory close by declaring that there was no other competent business.

That was the trouble with temporary principal teachers, Morris reflected inwardly. They had no real *commitment* to the job, no real understanding of how to make a team pull together. It was probably going to be the same with the history department this session as well, he thought to himself: Miss Denver, the department's principal teacher, had commenced her maternity leave in the first week of September, an admirable feat of family planning which had ensured her summer holiday was spent on full-service employment – and

14

pay. Two weeks after her return, she had left with a gift from the staff and suffused with a rosy glow of infanticipation.

Left behind to pick up the pieces was Martin Henderson, the only other member of the history department. Like Simon Young before him, he set to the task with unbridled enthusiasm. Like Simon Young before him, he calculated that a promoted post, albeit on a temporary basis, could only lead to better things in the long term. It was not long before reality overtook him in the guise of preparations for Standard grade.

In the meantime, Morris turned his attention to his hopes for the school board election. The school board initiative, he reckoned, would be an exciting challenge, a chance for teachers and parents to work together for the ultimate benefit of the school. And once on the board, he pondered, there would be a chance to exercise some real power and, mayhap, suggest some alterations to the composition of the supposedly mixed-ability classes in the first year. Sad to relate, however, Morris was not experiencing top-level support for a board nomination, as his diary entry for the end of September will amply testify . . .

Monday

My attempts to become staff representative on the new school board continue to meet with resistance from the headmaster, who appears determined to block my chances. For a start, he seems unwilling to accept that no other member of staff wishes to have anything to do with this extension of parental democracy, and told me today that he plans to hold a secret ballot for our two staff places.

'A secret ballot, Mr Ross?' I queried. 'But who are the other candidates?'

'Um . . .' he parried. 'Eh . . . can't tell you that, Simpson. Wouldn't be a secret then, would it?'

Before I could refute his logic he had turned and retreated to the confines of his study.

I begin to wonder if it's still worth my while standing for election, but feel that at least one member of staff has to give a good impression to the parents on the board – particularly given the example of rectorial ineffeciency so far demonstrated by Mr Ross in his organisation of the initial ballots for parents.

Despite his protestations about not having been trained for menial clerical tasks, his embarrassment has been immense: to begin with, he bought a cheap batch of wholesale envelopes to send out the ballot forms, all of which turned out to be too small for the necesssary papers without their being folded into several cramped and bulky packages; additionally, his timesaving scheme for using the Christmas leavers to address envelopes meant that no proper check was kept of the addressees. Unfortunately, two hundred sets of parents received three ballot forms each, while others received none at all; additionally, over three hundred forms went out to parents of pupils who had left school in the past two years, and who were consequently ineligible to vote.

Mr Pickup suggested that the entire affair was a disgrace to the school, and that the headmaster would have been better employed in trying to organise a Sunday School picnic: '– if that wouldn't be beyond him as well! Quite honestly, Simpson,' he confronted me this morning, 'D'you really *want* to serve on a board that has John Ross on it – even if he *is* a non-voting member?'

I told him I did, and I would. And I shall.

Tuesday

Today saw the return of Tommy McShane from his second suspension within four weeks of starting secondary school: to date, he has received only one and a half complete days of education at Parkland High. If his behaviour during my English class this morning was anything to go by, it struck me that it wouldn't be long before he was forbidden the opportunity to come to school once more. And so it proved.

I had been irritated for some several minutes during my reading of a haunting Walter de la Mare poem by the tinny sounds of a transistor radio in the distance. Or so I thought, until I raised my eyes from the anthology to discover the bold McShane nodding his head and snapping his fingers to the insistent beat of a set of personal stereo headphones.

'McShane!' I bellowed. 'Get those things off at once!'

He pretended not to hear so I repeated the command, this time standing directly in front of his desk. The ignorant little tyke continued snapping his fingers, so I lowered myself to his direct line of vision and, once again, shouted my insistence that he remove the offending headphones at once.

'Whit?' he shouted over the music pounding into his eardrums. 'Whit ye say? Canny heer ye.'

'Get them off, McShane. At once!' I commanded.

He seemed to hear that request all right. Taking advantage of a *double entendre* apparent to only the most salacious of minds, he immediately cast the headphones to his desk and started to remove several items of clothing, much to the amusement of the rest of his class. Fortunately, the bell went before he could complete his performance, and I was able to laugh the matter off without, I think, losing too much face.

Not so Mr Pickup. He encountered the selfsame musical interruptions to his religious education lesson on the Beatitudes this afternoon. Having issued an instruction to McShane to remove the headphones at once – and having met with the same dumb insolence as myself this morning – he then proceeded to attempt their removal himself. At which point McShane jumped to his feet and told Pickup in exactly which part of his professorial anatomy the headphones would end up if he so much as laid a finger on them.

Pickup, of course, is not so adept as me at dealing with difficult children. Without further ado, he had the boy suspended for another fortnight with immediate effect.

I am beginning to wonder if this is what McShane actually *wants*.

Wednesday

Graham Taylor returned today from his three week holiday in Scarborough. In fact, it turned out to be a four week holiday because – as his mother put it in her note of explanation – the 'wether was so rare that we staid on a bit'.

Needless to say, he had attempted none of the homework which his mother had demanded he be given before departure, and which had cost me no little time in preparation.

Such parental encouragement to miss out on valuable schooling time, however, paled into insignificance before Craig Stewart's announcement, during my fourth year class this afternoon, that he was 'off to Magalluf fur a month wi' ma folks.'

'You must be joking!' I berated him. 'This is your fourth year, Craig. Your Standard grade year. You'll miss out on an entire section of the course for your exam, and you won't be able to have any assessments made until –'

'Tough shit –' was his carefully considered reply. 'Ma' dad says the hoalidays ur cheepur the now. Don't wet yursel, Misturr Simpsun. Ah'll send yees all a postcard – awright?'

Words failed me. It's difficult enough trying to teach Standard grade English when the department's most up-to-date set of practice material is a set of 1976 O grade papers. And when pupils like Stewart display such a complete lack of concern for their examination courses, I really wonder if it's worth my while bothering.

Thursday

My concerns about preparations for Standard grade English were thrown into sharp relief this afternoon during a conversation with Martin Henderson, our acting head of history. He informed me that our own troubles were as nothing compared with those of the history department.

'Listen, Simpson,' he confided outside the history storecupboard this afternoon. 'If any of *my* pupils were off to Magalluf, I'd be more than willing to personally escort them to the airport; at least there'd be one less set of assessements to mark for October – and one less set of course material to duplicate.'

'Mmm,' I agreed. 'You certainly seem to be spending a lot of time in the photocopying room these days, Martin. It must be using up a fair amount of your requisition cash?'

'Fair amount? Hah! It uses up the entire bloody lot! Have you *seen* the course material they've sent out from the central support groups?'

I admitted my ignorance, so he threw open the storecupboard doors: 'Look at it,' he waved an arm across several thousand sheets of Standard grade history resources, all neatly packaged in cellophane bundles. 'Biggest waste of paper since the Munich agreement. And that's just the start,' he warned me. 'I've still to make class sets of each sheet, which should keep us going until Christmas, or so they tell me. For next term –' and here he struggled with an enormous parcel from the second shelf – 'they've given us a collection of worksheets that makes *War and Peace* look like a short story by Jeffrey Archer.'

I expressed surprise at the prodigious amount of coursework, but suggested that at least he should be grateful for so much assistance with his lesson preparation.

'Hah!' he exclaimed. ' That's all very well, but d'you know when this lot arrived?'

Again, I expressed uncertainty.

'First batch, end of June; second batch, end of August. Hardly gives us much time to bone up on it all, does it? At the moment I'm about two worksheets ahead of the third year – and they're catching up fast.'

'Well it does seem –' I began to sympathise, but by now Henderson was in full flow:

'And another thing,' he staggered into the corridor with the latest batch of curricular materials loaded between his arms. 'Come into my room and see just how many – AAARGH! You stupid wee buggers! Come here at once!'

I stepped quickly into the corridor to discover Henderson buried beneath an awesome mountain of paper which had fallen to the floor, shouting vainly in the direction of some first year boys with whom he had just collided.

'Catch them, Simpson!' he spluttered from the floor. ' Little towrags were running a relay race down the corridor –'

I gave chase, but was too late to identify the culprits. The only one I thought I could see was Tommy McShane, but I must have been mistaken: he's still under suspension, after all.

I reported the unsuccessful chase to Henderson.

'Never mind,' he accepted the failure philosphicaly enough and started to pick himself from the floor. 'Just give us a hand to gather this lot up, will you? Then we'll have to get them all into order, and start – AARGH!' he interrupted himself for the second time in quick succession. 'Bloody hell! I don't believe it . . .'

I asked what was the matter.

'No page numbers . . .' his voice shook disbelievingly, as he held a worksheet to my face. 'They've not put on any page numbers. Nine hundred and forty three sheets, and not a page number amongst them! How can I get them back in order?'

I skimmed through a handful of worksheets and confirmed the cause of his distress. A great deal of interesting material but now, alas, arranged in an irredeemably disorganised fashion. Henderson had started a quiet sobbing by now, so I thought it best to gather the worksheets as best possible, lock them in the storecupboard, and suggest a few pints at four o'clock. He seemed touched by my concern, and was happy to join me. Pickup came along as well, to lend a sympathetic ear.

Friday

The headmaster has found another staff candidate for the school board, but still needs another one to hold an election. As yet, nobody else seems interested.

Unfortunately, the new candidate is none other than Andrew Crichton, our school janitor. Without wishing to sound dismissive of the man's undoubted abilities in certain areas, I am unhappy to think that our future board's discussions on whole-school policies might be hijacked by our irascible little janitor holding forth on requisition moneys for school toilet paper, the lack of which appears to be a constant source of concern for him.

Be that as it may, it looks as if we are likely to be unopposed in our intentions of serving on the board. Personally, I look forward to the challenge.

Meanwhile, Martin Henderson's worries about the Standard grade history worksheets have been eased considerably. I dropped into his classroom this afternoon to offer further sympathy and a willingness to assist in the re-sorting of materials.

'Ah. Thanks a lot, Morris,' he smiled. 'But not necessary.'

'No? What have you done with them? Burned the lot?'

He laughed. 'Nothing quite so drastic, I'm pleased to say. In fact, it turned out to be an ideal source of investigative work for the third year this morning. Got them all to pretend they were secret agents trying to decode impenetrable signals during the second world war. Good bit of empathy there,' he sniggered. 'Told them these sheets were all mixed up, and each group had to get its own section in the right order. Took them all morning, but they did it. And gave *me* a chance to get a bit further ahead of them on the coursework, too,' he concluded triumphantly.

'And what about the page numbers?' I asked. 'Have you done anything about them, in case it happens again?'

'All taken care of, Morris,' he smiled again. 'Come and see.'

And so saying, he led me off to the home economics department. Briefly, he explained, he'd at last found a task which was suited to the abilities of the Christmas leavers, currently enjoying an afternoon block of social and vocational skills with Miss Tarbet. Proudly, he swung open the door of Room A36 to reveal a veritable hive of industry. Each of its twelve occupants was equipped with a large, thick, black felt pen and was laboriously entering consecutive page numbers on each worksheet of Henderson's Standard grade history courses.

'Now,' chuckled Henderson proudly, '*that's* what I call inter-departmental liaison!'

20

October

It is a truth aknowledged that teachers' holidays are far too long.

Acknowledged, that is, by everyone except the teachers.

They say, with some justification, that their job has such endemic levels of stress that regular – and lengthy – periods of recuperation are an essential component of their working year. They say, again with some justification, that most of the parents who make such complaints about their length of holidays never witness the hours of unseen preparation and course planning which goes on during these holidays.

And, perhaps most justified point of all, they ask why – if the school holidays are so inordinately long – do increasing numbers of parents nowadays find it impossible to take a family holiday *during* this period, instead of choosing to disrupt their children's carefully structured education? For many pupils, the October Week becomes an October Fortnight, with some taking an extra few days of leisure before the official holiday, some a few extra days after it.

And some, like Craig Stewart, took both. Morris Simpson considered it a disgrace, and a closer adherence to official holiday arrangements was just one of the topics which he planned to raise after his successful election to Parkland High's school board.

Because, strange to tell, Morris had actually been elected to the board during the penultimate week of October. He was unopposed, it is true, and there had been some difficulty in locating a second member of staff once Mr Crichton had withdrawn his name from the frame, but elected he was.

Morris looked forward to the challenge. There was so much to do, so many new avenues of influence to cultivate. Secretly, he hoped for an eventual position as chairman of the board, but that could wait: for just now, he looked ahead to one of the topics dearest to his heart – liaison with the local feeder school, Parkland Primary. In particular, he wanted to intiate a much greater degree of co-operation with Miss Hatfield (the primary school's headmistress) about the use of certain textbooks which were also being utilised by his own English department, not to mention his own private concern over the junior school curriculum.

His diary entry for October illustrates the problems . . .

Monday

At last, as a fully fledged member of our new school board, I look forward to our first meeting next month. Fortunately, the school janitor decided not to go ahead with his plan to become the other staff representative: Mr Crichton withdrew his nomination upon making the discovery that overtime payments would not, after all, be made available for attending board meetings. Conversely, my colleague from religious education and geography, Mr Pickup, decided at the last moment to allow his name to go forward as the other sole staff nominee.

I congratulated him upon at last having the interests of the school at heart; his reply that such service would look 'pretty good on the next job application' led me to suspect that his motives, as usual, owe more to blatant self-interest than to educational altruism. Nevertheless, I think we should make a formidable 'staff team' on the board: it's very exciting to be part of the school's new democratic accountability to the community it seeks to serve.

Tuesday

Craig Stewart, from my Standard grade class, returned today from his three week sojourn in Majorca, a liberal extension of the week's October break to which the rest of us were entitled.

He remains completely unconcerned about the fact that he has missed two pieces of folio assessment work; indeed, he seemed more intent upon regaling his classmates with lurid tales about the excessive daily quantities of lager he managed to consume during the 'Magalluf Happy-Hour' than with catching up on missed work. I questioned him about his parents' reactions to such illicit goings-on, but he informed me that they, in their turn, were 'permanently tanked-up, surr', and were consequently little interested in the activities of their wayward son.

Sometimes I wonder what the world's coming to.

Of more immediate concern to me than Craig Stewart's incipient alchoholism, however, is the reaction of my first year pupils to their new class reader. I had been looking forward to sharing their enthusiasm for a delightful story of youthful endeavour and spirited determination. Sadly, I had just concluded my stirring introduction to *The Silver Sword* by distributing copies from the front of the class when Janie Carswell – one of the brighter and better-spoken pupils in the grouping – wailed a disappointed cry of rejection across the room:

'Aw, sir – we've *done* this book already.'

'Sorry, Janie?' I enquired. 'How d'you mean?'

'We've *done* it, sir. In primary school . . .'

'What – you mean you've already read it?'

'Yes – and so's everybody else. Mrs Allan read it to us in Primary Five.' The rest of the class chorused in agreement.

'Ah,' I countered. 'So you've only had it *read* to you, then. You haven't done any *work* around it?'

Janie's nose wrinkled in distaste: 'Work?' she questioned, as if she'd never heard of the word.

'Yes, work,' I enlarged. 'You know: a theme study; associated poems; integrated literature; group activities connected to the book's central theme . . .'

I think I lost her at some point, because her face clouded over.

23

'Aw, sir,' she bleated, 'don't spoil it. I thought it was just a good story. For primary five,' she added pointedly.

I closed the discussion by explaining that there were no alternative readers in the storecupboard, and telling them that they would get *much* more out of the story now that they were older and more able to appreciate its finer points.

Janie didn't look convinced. I'm sure she'll change her mind when she starts my project theme study on Thursday.

Wednesday

A bitter confrontation between the English and modern languages departments this afternoon. The conflict arose as Jack Ferguson, principal teacher of modern languages, was marking some of the first year French assessments in the staffroom:

'God almighty!' he broke forth, as he failed yet another contribution from one of his pupils. 'Why the hell can't they write in proper paragraphs these days? Don't you lot teach them *anything* in English, Simon?'

My temporary principal teacher, Simon Young, raised his pencil from a newspaper crossword, and asked for elucidation.

'This lot from 1P,' criticised Mr Ferguson: 'they can't write in paragraphs properly. I'm fed up of failing essays that –'

'Paragraphs?' interrupted Simon. 'Well, of course not. Not if that's a first year class. Paragraphs are part of their second year course.'

'You what?' stuttered Jack Ferguson. 'You mean I'm marking them down on poor paragraphing and you're not even teaching them how to do it in the first place?'

'Certainly not. We've quite enough trouble on our hands making sure they master the sentence properly by the end of first year. We can hardly complicate matters further by –'

'Oh, for God's sake. And what about direct speech? I've been slashing marks off all over the place because I can't understand who's supposed to be speaking in their half-baked ruddy stories. I suppose you don't teach them *that* until second year either?'

'No, no,' corrected Simon. 'Direct speech punctuation is part of their *third* year syllabus. In fact,' he continued, oblivious to Jack Ferguson's reddening features, 'we actively discourage them from using direct speech until then. Over half of them get terribly confused by it all, and we frequently recommend that –'

'And what about the other half that *doesn't* get confused by it all?'

barked Ferguson, brandishing a jotter aloft. 'Look at this: Janie Carswell could write a tremedous essay from the day she walked into this place. I've been trying to figure out why she's gone downhill over the last few months, and now it all becomes clear. She's stopped punctuating her work correctly because the English department's misguided egalitarianism means she's to be dragged into the gutter along with the rest of the illiterate dregs who make up 1P – and probably,' he added *sotto voce*, 'along with half of the sodding English department as well.'

Simon began to make a spirited defence of current teaching practice within his department which involved a heated and angry exchange of views, and which was finally concluded with Ferguson's shouted asserertion that 'half of the damned first year wouldn't know a noun from an adjective, or a past participle from a future perfect . . .'

'No!' bellowed Simon, angry in return. 'And a bloody good thing too!'

I confess to a certain sympathy for Mr Ferguson's viewpoint, but departmental loyalty demanded my continued silence on the matter. However, perhaps I should let Janie Carswell go back to using paragraphs, after all . . .

Thursday

The *Silver Sword* project got off to a rather poor start with 1P this afternoon, mainly due to Janie Carswell's unyielding obstinacy, ably supported by the rest of the class.

My initial suggestion that the class begin the lesson by designing a colourful cover for the book was howled down by the communal complaint that they had spent 'all morning in Art daein' book cuvvers'. My alternative idea to produce a newspaper article based on the events in the first chapter was countered with the objection that they had all 'done a newspaper article in modern studies' only yesterday.

And so the argument went on: I suggested an improvised dialogue based on a radio interview; they'd already done that in drama. I suggested writing a letter to an imaginary friend abroad; they'd already done that in French. I suggested a role-play based on the historical events in Chapter 2; they'd done role-plays in history last week. I suggested composing a song lyric about the book's main characters; they'd already written songs – and accompanying music – in music.

Honestly. I wish other departments would keep to teaching their *own* subjects, and leave the English department to teaching English.

Friday

Mentioned the problem with the first year reader to Simon Young at break this morning.

'Bloody primary school,' he swore. 'That's the third time since Christmas that they've decimated the first year curriculum. Why, only last week I handed them over sixty-five copies of our previously most popular reader because half the year group had already done it in primary six. Miss Hatfield promised greater liaison in future – hah! Now another book bites the dust. If I could just –'

Our conversation was interrupted by a telephone call for me.

'Hello?' I greeted the anonymous caller. 'Morris Simpson speaking.'

'Simpson?' crackled a distant voice. 'Yes. You're the one. Good morning. Alan Carswell here.'

'Alan *who*?'

'Carswell. Janie's father.'

'Oh, good morning, Mr Carswell,' I answered, an inexplicable foreboding in my heart. 'And what can I do for you?'

'Well, Mr Simpson,' he spoke sharply: 'it's not so much what you can do for *me*, as what you can do for my daughter.'

'Oh? How d'you mean?'

'I mean, Mr Simpson, that I'm more than a little disappointed at the standard and quality of work expected of her in Parkland High – and most especially the work expected of her in the English department.'

'But surely –'

'It seems to me,' he continued, oblivious of my attempts to speak, 'that you seem intent upon undoing seven years' work by Parkland Primary in teaching her to write with due regard for the normal rules of the English language.'

I denied the charge strenuously, but Mr Carswell carried on regardless: 'And not content with that,' he launched a further attack, 'you seem happy to re-cycle ancient books which Parkland Primary has been using for years, books which –'

I began to tell him that this was an exact reversal of the true situation, but he had the bit between his teeth by now. To cut a long story short, a very one-sided conversation ensued, during the course of which Mr Carswell questioned my professional authority, capability and judgement in several ways and no uncertain manner. Ultimately, he left me with little choice other than to tell him that I had better things to do with my time than speak to jumped-up, ill-mannered and objectionable parents whose idea of a professional consultation was to hurl unfounded accusations down a telephone line. Then I rang off.

'There,' I finished in satisfaction as I recounted the conversation to Mr Pickup some minutes later. 'I told him where to get off. I don't think I'll be hearing from *him* for some time.'

'On the contrary,' Pickup corrected me. 'I think you might just get the opportunity to carry on your discussion at some future occasion.'

'I doubt it, Pickup,' I smiled. 'I've no intention of crossing *his* path again.'

'Morris,' explained Pickup patiently, a hand on my shoulder. 'Have you seen the results of the parental ballot for the school board yet?'

'No, but –'

Suddenly Pickup's meaning became clear. My voice shook. 'He's not . . . he's not . . . on it, is he?'

Pickup nodded sadly. 'Highest number of votes among all the parent members, apparently. A very popular – and influential – man, by all accounts . . .'

Suddenly, democracy doesn't seem such a wonderful thing.

November

Apart from the unwelcome news of Mr Carswell's place on the school board, there were clearly many concerns which clouded Morris Simpson's educational horizons that autumn. There had been, however, one mitigating factor to date: the almost constant absence of Tommy McShane from his class.

Tommy McShane had spent seven years in primary school. During the first four of these years, his young body had been subject to a wide variety of unusual and imaginative illnesses, the sudden advent of which would: (a) bewilder medical opinion; (b) cause much distress to his parents; and (c) ensure that he need not attend school for long periods of time.

By the time Tommy reached Primary 5, his creativity was hard put to find new illnesses with which to abscond himself from school, and the McShane family doctor was beginning to lose patience with a child whom he had long since correctly identified as a school phobic.

Tommy took, instead, to playing truant on every conceivable occasion: his attendance record during his last three years of primary schooling was abysmal, and Tommy spent many a happy hour in Parkland's shopping centre or – if funds permitted – in the local amusement arcade. There were, unfortunately, the associated problems of the attendance officers who insisted upon disturbing his parents (educational psychologists both) at their work, and Tommy had become weary of the family arguments which inevitably ensued.

As he approached secondary education, then, it was with a sudden epiphany of thought that he hit upon the ideal solution of an officially sanctioned, long-term holiday from school. The disciplinary system of most schools today hinges on the somewhat unusual premise that pupils will be prevented from coming to school if they behave badly enough to merit suspension. For some pupils, this will indeed be a source of abject embarrassment and shame; for others – like Tommy McShane – it is a passport to unlimited holidays and untrammelled leisure-time, with no worries about attendance officers trying to hasten unwilling pupils back to school. Twelve weeks into his first year of comprehensive education at secondary school, Tommy McShane had still to record two consecutive days in the place.

But in November, he was due back. Morris's column for that month recalls, among other things, the occasion of McShane's longest continuous attendance spell since August, as well as Parkland's approach – by no means unusual in large institutions – to the safe and efficient conduct of fire-drills. And, for the first time, the newly-convened school board of Parkland Community High was due to meet together. It was to be an historic occasion.

Monday

A busy week ahead, what with my first school board meeting, not to mention the return from further suspension of Tommy McShane, the ill-behaved lout from 1P, who has yet to record two consecutive days' attendance since August.

To cap it all, a large staffroom notice proclaimed that there would be a fire-drill at period three on Friday.

'But that's ridiculous,' I complained to Mr Major, the assistant headteacher (AHT) in charge of the affair, '– you can't *tell* people when there's going to be a fire drill!'

'Of course you can,' he countered swiftly, 'and,' he added needlessly, 'I've just done it. You try organising 500 people to get out of a building quickly and efficiently. Got to give them *some* warning, Simpson.'

'Well,' I replied, ' I thought the whole point of a fire-drill was to make people realise they don't *get* any warning with a real fire,' but I might as well have held my breath, for Major refused to countenance anything so haphazard as an unplanned fire-drill. I think he's very foolish.

Tuesday

Tommy McShane returned for his fourth day of secondary education today, and his arrival was marked by the addition of several notices to the guidance staff's 'early warning' remarks on the staffroom notice board. As the guidance teacher responsible for first year, Frank Parker's request seemed the most succinct, if a little indelicate: 'THOMAS MCSHANE,' it announced its subject in large black capitals: '– this boy is on permanent report. If he so much as breaks wind without permission, send him to me at once. I will crucify him.'

Whatever happened, I wonder, to the *caring* side of guidance?

Wednesday

Our first school board meeting tonight – and it augured poorly for the future, I'm afraid to report.

Our parental representatives seem an ill-assorted bunch comprising, amongst others, the prospective Conservative councillor for the next district elections, as well as a rather boorish man smelling strongly of drink and a demure little woman who laughed nervously at the slightest remark, no matter its content, humorous or not.

Mr Pickup and I – as staff representatives – felt singularly outnumbered and outflanked, particularly when the five parent members outvoted us in electing a chairman. This, unfortunately, turned out to be Mr Carswell, father of one of my first year pupils, and a man with whom I have already crossed swords concerning the content of our English curriculum.

His opening remarks set the tone for the evening.

'Right,' he announced. 'I take it you've all read the bumf we got sent out from the Scottish Education Department? Three hundredweight of useless wastepaper, as far as I'm concerned – they'd have been better leaving the forests standing that went to make up *that* lot. Am I right?'

Mrs Baird laughed nervously, while the rest of the board tried to obscure the fact that they had yet to examine the material in question.

'Well, it doesn't really make any difference,' Carswell relaunched himself. 'All that it keeps on about is the need to forge effective partnerships between parents and staff in the business of running the school. Well, as far as I'm concerned, that's a load of old balls!'

Mr Ross, as observing headmaster, opened his mouth to speak, but choked back a response as he recalled his position of impotence.

'This place,' continued Carswell, 'needs a good shaking up, and it's our job to do the shaking,' he explained, with a pointed glance in my direction.

On he went, oblivious to Pickup's attempts to interrupt. In short, Mr Carswell seemed to be of the opinion that Parkland High School has been failing in its duty to educate the district's youth. He outlined a fearsome agenda for the coming months, including such topics as the reintroduction of compulsory school uniform for all year-groups, the re-insertion of class placings in report cards and, finally, the removal of certain 'objectionable' texts from the English curriculum.

I thought I saw my opportunity here, but he forestalled me again.

'And no, Mr Simpson, I don't mean the regurgitated primary-school novels that I was on to you about last month.'

'No?' I queried.

'No,' he replied. 'It's more serious than that. I've been investigating some of the senior reading material that you lot put in front of our kids, and I must say I've been horrified!'

Again, he set forth on a vindictive diatribe, this time directed at the English department. In short, his argument centred on the fact that there are several texts used by the department with fourth, fifth and sixth year pupils which contain what he chose to describe as 'purple prose and pornographic filth'. He was unwilling to admit my contention that *Cider With Rosie* and *Saturday Night and Sunday Morning*, among others, were seminal works of English literature.

On the contrary, he closed the meeting with his stated intention of 'going public' on the matter, and also of 'going through future textbook requisitions with a fine toothcomb.'

I wonder what he meant by 'going public'?

Thursday

The fire-drill has been moved to period five tomorrow, owing to the petitions of the home economics department, who claimed it would 'spoil the second year's sponge cakes to leave them unattended'.

Honestly – I hope a real fire would be as considerate.

The office contacted me during afternoon break to say there was a reporter from the local paper on the telephone; he wanted a word with me about the controversy over textbooks in the English department, but I refused to speak to him.

Friday

Horrific confusion over the fire-drill this morning.

To start with, I was unsettled by having my period three class moved up to Floor C, while some essential roof repairs were carried out on my own room in the outside huts. Then, having just begun a poetry reading with 1P at the start of the period, I was dismayed to have the lesson interrupted by the harsh jangling of what the pupils took to be a fire alarm.

'No, no,' I shouted over the ringing bells. 'It's not until period five – that must be a call for the janitor or something.'

They took some convincing, but I got them settled back into their seats eventually, and carried on with my poetry reading. However, I began to doubt my own words as the bells continued to screech a message whose import was finally confirmed by the furious features of Mr Major putting his head round the door.

'Simpson!' he bellowed. 'What the hell d'you think you're doing?'

'But surely,' I stammered, 'the fire alarm's not until period five? What about Miss Tarbet's cakes?'

'Bugger Miss Tarbet's cakes!' he shouted back, with no sense of propriety for the first year whatsoever. 'This is a *real* fire, Simpson!'

'What!' I screeched. 'Why didn't you say so? Everybody out!'

In retrospect, perhaps I should have been calmer. Alas, my words seemed to inflame the situation, as thirty two members of 1P – mercifully devoid of Tommy McShane who had failed to turn up for the lesson – all rushed to the door together. Mr Major was bundled unceremoniously aside as the class headed pell-mell for the nearest staircase. Miraculously, they appeared to reach the bottom without major disaster, but it was an object lesson in how *not* to evacuate a building, as Mr Major was quick to forcibly point out as I helped him up from the floor and we scurried downstairs ouselves.

Fortunately, the fire was not serious, and turned out to be a minor conflagration in the English storecupboard, which was soon extinguished by the local fire brigade. Sadly, about half of our book-store was destroyed – news which will no doubt hearten Mr Carswell of the school board.

In fact, I wondered at one point if he had had anything to do with the affair, because by lunchtime the news around the school was that the fire had been started deliberately and would be the subject of police investigation – or, as Pickup inevitably informed us: 'there's been arson about'.

Suddenly, I began to ponder anew the question of Tommy

McShane's wherabouts during period three, when he was supposed to be with me . . .

By afternoon, the whole sorry tale was out. The fire had not, in fact, been started deliberately, but young McShane – bored by four uneventful days at school – had chosen to spend most of the morning in the English storecupboard with a packet of Embassy King-Size and a box of matches. A careless cigarette-end – his fifth of the day, as forensic evidence later revealed – coupled with his removal to the first-year toilets for natural relief, had conspired to start the fire which signalled Tommy's most serious and lengthy suspension to date. We shall not see him again until after Christmas.

Sadly, the day ended on an even worse note. I was standing at the bus stop, looking forward with obvious relief to the weekend, when my eye chanced to catch the newsagent's hoarding for the *Parkland Gazette*. Disbelieving at first, I had to look again to make sure that my first reading had been correct.

Sure enough: there it was, in hastily scrawled letters across the advertisement for today's edition:

**'Parkland High School
– Sex Books Scandal –
English Teacher Denies Accusations!'**

I hunched my head between my shoulders and, with a sinking feeling in the pit of my stomach, boarded the bus home.

December

It would be incorrect to give the impression that all school boards were as aggressively involved as Parkland High's. In some schools the boards tended to become administrative organisations whose sole purpose was the official approval of whatever decisions had already been taken on their behalf by the school management. Others became more involved in debating the pros and cons of weighty educational concerns such as school lets and roof repairs. And a few – such as Parkland's – decided to utilise their newly authorised powers in a manner which could only be described as interfering.

It will already have become apparent that Morris had chosen an unfortunate enemy in the board chairman, Alan Carswell: his distress had been great on learning of Carswell's disclosures to the local press, but he determined that it would not affect his enthusiasm for the pioneering work of the board. Indeed, he even displayed enough initiative to use the *Parkland Gazette* report in a media studies unit with his fourth year class, by letting them compare his own version of the story with the newspaper's, and allowing them to draw their own conclusions about the distorting power of the press.

Craig Stewart, alas, seemed to miss the point of the lesson, for he spent an industrious half-hour during the lunchbreak scouring Morris's classroom for the 'sex manuals' which he plainly understood his English teacher to possess. 'It must be troo, surr,' he responded when challenged by Morris to explain his ferreting purposes: '– it sed so in the paypurr!'

Concerned lest any more such indelicate rumours should begin circulation, Morris engaged the services of a local solicitor, to which end he hoped the flames of gossip could be swiftly extinguished. Other than this, he was looking forward to his Christmas holidays. Between pupil misbehaviour, intransigent parents and unexpected conflagrations, he felt that he needed a break. His diary entry for December has a weary air about it.

Monday

The final week of term – on Thursday we break up for Christmas, and Thursday can't come soon enough as far as I'm concerned. I have never known a term which has given me so many problems, both in terms of everyday classroom discipline and the ever increasing mountains of administrative work. Teaching seems to come very low on the prioroty list, I'm afraid.

At least the school's adverse publicity surrounding the books studied and used by the English department seems to have abated. After the school board's chairman 'went public' over his criticisms last month, I have had an embarrassing few weeks (as one of the board's staff representatives) denying the claims of local journalists that Parkland High – in using classic texts like *Cider With Rosie* and *Billy Liar* - is engaged in a seditious plot to corrupt the morals of the district's youth.

Eventually, my solicitor advised me to make no further comment on the matter and, sure enough, the fuss seems to have died down. It looks as if I shan't have to worry about it any more – which is more than can be said for my solicitor's bill. Talk about money for old rope . . .

Tuesday

I spoke too soon.

Mr Pickup, who has taken to reading *The Sun* as well as *The Guardian* of late – he claims he finds the former's crosswords more approachable – arrived in school with a broad grin creasing his features.

'Morning, Morris,' he smiled, slapping two folded newspapers on to the staffroom coffee table. 'The national press now, is it? Fame at last, old son?'

Uncertain of his drift, I lifted *The Guardian* to see what he meant, only to discover a lurid tabloid headline on the front of the paper beneath:

SCHOOLKIDS IN HARD-CORE CURRICULUM SHOCKER!

Horrified, I turned to what constituted the 'story' behind this three-quarter page banner, only to discover a barely literate, sensationalist rewriting of the report which had already appeared in last month's *Parkland Gazette*, suggesting that the books we used contained passages of more than dubious taste – except that this time our English department had been collectively termed a 'gang of sex-mad school-teachers with only one thing on their tiny minds'. It's hardly very fair to Mr Major, soon to be knocking on retirement's door – or indeed to any of us, come to think of it.

The school board chairman, for his part, was decribed as 'anxious Alan Carswell – champion of Parkland's Ban the Bawdy Books Campaign!'

I'm going to have this out with Carswell, and have asked for the matter to be put on the agenda for tomorrow evening's school board meeting.

Wednesday

An awful day.

Much of the morning was taken up with avoiding a posse of press photographers who appeared to have set up a base camp just outside the playground. The headmaster, for his part, had to deal with a barrage of telephone calls from over-inquisitive reporters and over-anxious parents, most of whose fears he managed to allay.

Personally, I tried to keep a low profile and spent the afternoon making quiet preparations for a small Christmas party I'm having with my first year class tomorrow, though I also took some time to prepare a statement on behalf of the staff for this evening's board meeting.

Sadly, Mr Carswell chose to ignore our collective thoughts on his unsettling chairmanship of the school board, and instead announced his intention to reject Simon Young's recently presented requisition for books which he required to replace those damaged in last month's stock-cupboard fire.

Wielding a large black felt pen, he struck several texts from Simon's list, including, among others, *A Pair of Jesus Boots* (which he described as blasphemous), a set of poems by Roger McGough ('pure filth'), as well as a class-set of George Mackay Brown's *Greenvoe* ('far too earthy'), despite this latter's status as a set text for the new Higher grade examination.

My own protests, on behalf of the English department, were brushed aside by Carswell who unbelievably seemed to have the support of all the other parent representatives on the board.

'No way, Mr Simpson,' he rebuffed my request to reconsider. 'We aim to clean up this cess-pit once and for all – understand?'

Mr Ross, as observing headmaster, shuddered quietly and put his head in his hands. He took me aside after the meeting, thanked me for my efforts, and announced that he thought it unnecessary for him to attend any future board meetings.

So much for parental partnership.

Thursday

The last day of term. I tried to put aside all thoughts of school board disharmony and media misrepresentation; instead, I made a conscious effort to get into the Christmas spirit. All went well until a late afternoon brush with Mr Tod, our depute head.

To explain, I had put a good deal of effort into organising class 1P's Christmas party first thing after lunch, my only teaching period of the afternoon. I started off by playing a recording of T S Eliot's *Journey of the Magi* (which, in retrospect, seemed a little beyond the first year) and then dished out some party hats and crisps before starting a game of charades.

It all seemed to be going well but, as usual, it only takes one person to spoil it for everyone: Alan McLeary – who appears to have taken on the role of class troublemaker during the continued suspension of Tommy McShane – chose an entirely inappropriate and extremely vulgar mime, complete with sound effects, to convey the film title *of Gone With The Wind*. The class seemed to think it hilarious, as did McLeary. However, I soon wiped the smile off his face:

'McLeary,' I bellowed, '– if you're going to make such offensive gestures – not to mention unpleasant odours – you can do it in the solitary confines of my cupboard – and you'll stay there till the end of the period!'

So saying, I directed him into my storecupboard, turned the key and pocketed it, lest any of his friends saw fit to spring an escape. In fact they all seemed to think it a hilarious response on my part, and the party went off without any further dispute. I think I even went up in their estimation as a result of my prompt response.

It all seemed a happy way to finish the term, I reflected in the staff-room during the last period of the day; indeed, after all the tribulations of recent weeks, I was more than happy to accept Pickup's offer of a Christmas refreshment at four o'clock in The Pig and Whistle. Unfortunately, we were just setting foot out of the front door when the extremely agitated figure of our depute head appeared on the horizon, accompanied by the school's senior cleaning lady.

'Simpson!' he bawled across the entrance hall. 'Have *you* got your storecupboard key? Mrs Young's been looking all over –'

'Storecupboard key, Mr Tod?' I called over. 'I don't think I've – oh my good God! Alan McLeary!'

'Yes, Mr Simpson,' he bustled over to me. 'There seems to be a child in some distress in your storecupboard. Wouldn't know anything about it, would you? Mrs Young was just clearing up the aftermath of your little festive celebrations,' – and here Mrs Young threw me a very disapproving glance – 'when she heard a despairing cry for assistance from your cupboard. And somebody seems to have removed the key . . . ?' He looked enquiringly at me.

I mumbled a brief explanation of McLeary's presence in the cupboard and followed up with an excuse about the boy being a vicious little brute. However, Tod suggested that – no matter the provocation – our disciplinary powers did not yet extend to enforced incarceration in storecupboards over the Christmas holidays. I handed him the key without further ado and was on hand to witness the release of a very emotional Alan McLeary.

The boy's face hardened, however, when he saw me. In a vitriolic outburst of surprising force for one so young, he accused me of several unmentionable character defects and promised future vengeance.

I decided that an apology was in order, but he was unwilling to accept it.

'Up yoors – surr,' he gestured most disrespectfully, and left the classroom in high dudgeon. Mr Tod followed him. Ominously, he said nothing.

I'm glad it's the end of term.

Friday

A long lie, followed by an abortive trip into town for some last-minute Christmas shopping. Sadly, I failed to get any further than the local newsagents, where I called to pick up a newspaper.

Waiting for change, my eye ranged across the selection of other papers on offer. Suddenly, it was was caught by *The Sun*'s continued and unusual interest in matters educational, as proclaimed in its by now familiar manner. Alan McLeary's promises of retribution had been swiftly fulfilled, as the headline confirmed in even larger type than before:

'DIRTY-BOOKS' SCHOOL - NEW YOUNG-BOY-IN-CUPBOARD SCANDAL!

Embarrassed beyond belief, I bought a copy. Clearly, the wolf-pack outside the school had pounced on the tear-stained McLeary and asked for his side of the story. In what passed for investigative reporting, and without bothering to check on the veracity of his statements, they'd seen fit to print a pack of lies about the abnormal methods of sadistic punishment meted out by teachers at Parkland High. I couldn't believe my eyes – I thought these people were supposed to have a code of conduct?

Gazing in horrified disbelief at the report, my eye glanced across the rest of the front page as well. There, in the top coner – just next to a scantily clad, extremely leggy, and definitely female Father Christmas, was a listing of the other major journalistic attraction for the day: *'Twenty Things You Didn't Know About Schoolbooks These Days – A Christmas Shocker!'*

I decided to go home instead and heat up some old mince pies. Anything to make it feel more like Christmas . . .

January

GOOD RIDDANCE!!#

Brief though it was, the Christmas holiday afforded Morris a chance to recharge his batteries. He returned to school in January with his customary optimism, and it wasn't long before he found himself immersed in the day to day enthusiasm of devising new projects and lesson plans for the classes under his charge.

This, it must be said, was what Morris Simpson enjoyed most about his teaching career: the daily contact with innovative youth, whose perception and writing talents could frequently surprise him by their almost precocious maturity. As he was to be reminded, most forcibly, at the end of January.

Of course, it was difficult to remember the real joys of teaching at times. To begin with, there were the continuing troubles with the school board, whose next meeting was scheduled for the last week in January. And then there were the endless rounds of educational politics which served to constantly disrupt the smooth flow of education which Parkland tried to provide. Just when a system of teaching, an approach, a methodology would appear to have become accepted practice, someone would come up with an alternative system, a new approach, a better methodology. It has happened in so many curricular areas over the years: today's educational bandwagon will become tomorrow's out of date theory. Let a few years pass, however, and the original theory will soon be back in favour. It is an endless circumlocution which passes for educational progress: this time round, Mr Tod had been given cause for timetabling concern by the recent inclusion of modern languages as a 'core subject' in the Scottish curriculum; consequently, he was proposing a change in the length of periods at Parkland High. Certain members of staff – Morris Simpson included – were experiencing a strong sense of *déja vu* . . .

Monday

An early closure for a staff meeting, allegedly called for discussion on Mr Tod's new timetable proposals to accommodate the burgeoning quantity of subjects which are to constitute our future 'core curriculum'. Between the competing and compulsory demands of modern languages, mathematics, English, life-skills, work-skills, communication skills, and every other skill whose mastery seems essential to the fullest development of a child's personality these days, he has found it impossible to devise a workable timetable which fits within the confines of our present sixty-five minute period.

Consequently, he has suggested – if suggested is the correct word – that we move back to a school day comprising nine forty minute periods.

Predictably, the staff were unanimous in their condemnation of the proposals.

'It's ridiculous!' screeched Miss Tarbet of home economics. 'How d'you expect them to bake a cake in forty minutes – especially when they've taken the first ten minutes to trail in from registration?'

'Yes,' agreed Jack Ferguson from modern languages. 'And what about us? We've got a whole screed of lesson units divided up into sixty-five minute chunks – are we expected to change them now to satisfy some –'

Mr Tod interrupted to point out that the need for such a renewal of timetable arrangements had been largely caused by the inclusion of Mr Ferguson's 'bloody subject as a core element' in the first place, and reminding Mr Ferguson that *he* had been among the loudest complainants when we changed from forty to sixty-five minute periods some five years ago.

Ferguson countered with a jibe about 'making up the rules as you go along' which was, perhaps, a valid point. Tod seemed to have decided upon the eventual outcome of the discussion long before the meeting had started, and his list of 'sound educational reasons' to justify the change to a shorter period was just about as lengthy – if memory serves aright – as his equivalent list to justify an *extension* of period length all those years ago.

The wheel turns full circle.

Tuesday

A surprise visit has been announced for Friday by Miss Bowman, our English Adviser. As former principal teacher of the department, I think she's been trying to avoid 'sticking her nose in', as it were, while Simon Young settled into the job. After allowing him thirteen months in post, therefore – albeit still as a temporary principal teacher – Angela has decided to swoop upon the department for a 'curriculum review and initial moderation appraisal' – whatever that means.

'Well, whatever it means,' frowned Simon this afternoon as he put down the telephone, '– we'd better make damned sure we've got some pupils' writing on the walls.'

'Yes,' agreed Mr Major wholeheartedly. 'Even if we have to write it ourselves . . .'

I reserved comment. My own classroom's walls, needless to say, display a veritable profusion of creative writing and artistic endeavour by my charges. Inwardly, I pondered the chances of making a good impression with a few carefully devised thematic studies for the visit. Angela Bowman always had a soft spot for me, I think, and this could be a chance for career advancement.

Wednesday

Suspicions that Mr Tod's motives in calling last Monday's meeting were far removed from democratic intent were confirmed by the appearance of his 'draft timetable' for next session on the staffroom wall this morning. Unsurprisingly, it outlined a day of nine periods, forty minutes each, and a request for 'any constructive suggestions or detailed objections in writing' to be in his hands by Friday afternoon at the latest.

It's hardly what I would call a full consultation period, and Mr Pickup agreed: he called a full staff meeting at lunch-time to organise a 'people's revolt'. I declined his invitation to attend and, as it turned out, so did most of the staff, who recognise a lost cause when they see it. In any case, I had work to do in preparing a detailed outline of our new disciplinary and assessment procedures for the school board meeting tonight.

Sadly, I never got the chance to use it because this, the third school board meeting of the session, eventually collapsed in ignominious confusion.

The problems started after Mr Carswell had rejected Simon Young's textbook requisition for the second time running (again on the highly subjective grounds of 'decency and good taste'), and ruled that there would be no further discussion on the matter. He thereupon proposed we move on to the next item on the agenda, which proved to be (his own) long and detailed enquiry about the upkeep of the school's 'dux board'.

'Well, gentlemen?' he questioned Pickup and myself. 'As staff representatives, perhaps you could let us know what the plans are?'

Momentarily taken aback by this sudden assault, our mouths gaped open in silent uncertainty.

'Don't just sit there like goldfish!' he barked. 'The dux board in the entrance hall – what are you going to *do* about it?'

'Do about it, Mr Carswell?' intervened Mr Ross, present in his role as observing headmaster. 'What d'you mean, *do* about it?'

'Well, it's hideously out of date, isn't it? The last name on there was painted on in 1976 – why haven't you kept it up to date?'

'Oh I see,' laughed Mr Ross. 'Well, we haven't put any names on since 1976, Mr Carswell, because we haven't *had* a dux since then. We stopped –'

'You what?' snapped Carswell. 'What d'you mean, no dux since then?'

'Well, we don't have a dux because we don't have an order of merit in the sixth year.' More certain of his ground than at previous board meetings, Mr Ross began warming to his theme, eager to explain current educational practice. 'Modern methods of assessment preclude the necessity to arrange children in a rank-order of merit. We prefer to set them achievable tasks, give them specific, grade-related criteria to achieve success at their own level of ability, and –'

Carswell's eyes had glazed over, but he suddenly snapped an interruption: 'My God!' he exclaimed. 'No wonder this place is in such a state. Speak plain English, can't you? It all seems perfectly simple to me – you award the dux to the pupil who gets the best marks.

43

You give each child something to aim at, to fight for. You can't just –'

I interrupted quietly with the perfectly polite observation that if the chairman wished to make comment upon school assessment policy, it would assist matters greatly if he had even a nodding acquaintance with more up-to-date educational theories than those upon which his own education had been so obviously founded.

'And what the hell d'you mean by that?' he barked. 'By God, Mr Simpson, if you had half the education in your little finger that I'd had by the age of ten, then perhaps my daughter might be *getting* somewhere in English! To think that people like you lot,' – and here he glanced sharply at all three staff members – 'are in charge of educating the nation's youth!'

Silently, I looked at Pickup and Mr Ross. In a rare display of staff unanimity, we nodded quietly at each other and, as one man, rose to our feet and left the room. It was, I thought, an extremely dignified departure under the circumstances, marred only by Carswell's parting shout of 'Good riddance'.

Mr Ross has *definitely* refused to attend the next board meeting, and Pickup and I may find something else to do as well.

Thursday

Tommy McShane returned from suspension today. Again.

I tried not to make any mention of his reappearance in Class 1P, and concentrated instead upon the St Valentine Theme with which I'm hoping to impress Angela Bowman.

The class seemed quite excited by it all and, after a brief explanation of some of the traditions behind St Valentine's Day, I told them how the next fortnight would be spent in preparation for the big day: a selection of poems, short stories, and dramatic improvisations culminating in a wall display and a series of 'Project Folders' for each member of the class.

'And first of all,' I informed them brightly, 'you're going to make your own Valentine cards!'

A buzz of excitement passed around the room as I filled in the details: 'Not all at once, of course,' I added: 'I just want you to make a start on them today and, as the project continues, you can go back to adding to them, making up rhymes for them, decorating them and so on, whenever you've finished the work I've set for you on any particular day.'

It was a good idea, though I say so myself, because it meant there was a real *incentive* for them all to finish their work each day. Even Tommy McShane and Alan McLeary seemed taken by the notion, and set to with scissors, card, and much scratching of pens.

I think Angela Bowman will be mightily impressed with the results.

Friday

The Valentine project has been cancelled.

Not that Angela Bowman wasn't impressed, mark you: she said that it was a long time since she'd seen such an innovative collection of poetry from such a young class and, indeed, many of them had put a great deal of effort into beginning their Valentine cards, complete with protestations of undying affection for the lucky recipient on St Valentine's Day.

It was all spoiled, alas, by the over-enthusiastic efforts of McShane and McLeary. Displaying a hitherto unsuspected zeal for hard work, the two of them had spent an extremely productive evening last night and arrived before registration this morning armed with already completed Valentine cards for their intended recipients.

I tried to explain that they were really far too early but, for once, a small glimmer of enthusiasm and initiative seemed to have been lit in their faces. They looked so eager – it would have been unreasonable to discourage them, so I relented.

'O.K., boys,' I whispered conspiratorially. 'Hide them in the girls' desks. I won't look to see who's geting them.'

Upon reflection, perhaps a wiser teacher would have looked over the cards first. Susan Campbell, certainly, should have been protected from the claims of sexual prowess which McLeary had made for himself in the card which he sent, while Janie Carswell, for her part, displayed a commendable self-control upon reading the versification which Tommy McShane had composed on her behalf. Among the several proposals of sexual athletics which the grubby-minded little boy had suggested, there were at least seven items which I would have considered physically and anatomically impossible, not to mention illegal. Of the rest, only one would have been permissable, given the age of consent.

I tried, of course, to confiscate the cards but both girls considered them personal property and insisted upon taking them home to their parents. Especially Janie Carswell.

Needless to say, her damned father was on the telephone by lunch-time, requesting a complete run-down of the first-year English syllabus and demanding to know where it suggested the composition of lavatorial graffiti as a worthwhile writing activity.

I passed him on to Simon Young. After all, that's what he's being paid for.

February

As Morris has correctly pointed out, in referring Alan Carswell to his principal teacher, he was simply tracing a management line which suggested that those teachers in receipt of a higher salary than others should be prepared to take upon themselves the various burdens demanded by their respective positions.

However, this management structure is more normally called into play when dealing with recalcitrant pupils rather than parents. Should a teacher's own disciplinary methods prove inadequate to maintain order – and Morris's frequently did – then the next line of sanction becomes a written referral to the department's principal teacher. Sometimes, the nature of the offence involves the preparation of a further written report, this time to one of the guidance staff or perhaps to an assistant head teacher. Occasionally, yet further reports will be required for other members of the school management team, and most certainly for the associated gatherings of psychologists and social workers who will, inevitably, have become involved by now. They will, in turn, write their own reports, and will consequently require further written replies to their suggested means of remediation. Punishing an errant pupil is no simple task these days.

In many cases, of course, the referral halts at principal teacher stage: the pupil will go 'on report', a 'conduct card' will be issued to encourage future good behaviour, and the 'peer group pressure' to achieve good ratings on this card – it is claimed – will inevitably lead to behavioural improvements.

It was a system which worked better with some pupils – and teachers – than with others, and it was certainly a system which had as its lynch-pin the effectiveness of the principal teacher in charge. As Morris's diary for the end of February will reveal, the frequent absence of Simon Young on a multifarious range of in-service courses made the referral system just that little bit more difficult to operate. Especially when faced with a pupil like Alan McLeary, who seemed completely incapable of accepting responsibility for the consequences of his own actions . . .

Monday

More disciplinary problems with the first year. Alan McLeary – already on report for his part in a vulgar prank during my St Valentine's project last month – spent a disruptive half-hour during this morning's poetry lesson with a constant stream of ill-mannered interruptions to my carefully prepared lesson plan. He was also, with two of his colleagues, instrumental in an attempt to cause serious injury to Janie Carswell: between them, they conspired to remove a chair from beneath the unfortunate girl as she was about to sit down.

At least I was able to exact some kind of revenge when McLeary presented me with a conduct card for signing at the end of the lesson. I ticked all three boxes marked 'Well Below Average' for each area of behaviour, effort and performance, all of which assessments meant a further immediate referral to Simon Young, my principal teacher.

Infuriatingly, the boy chose to challenge my comments on his behaviour.

'Aw, surr!' he drawled. 'That's no' ferr!'

'What d'you mean, McLeary? It's pefectly fair!'

'It's no', surr – ah wis guid a' moarnin', so ah wis.'

I couldn't believe my own ears. In addition to the comprehensive evidence of my own eyes, I had sworn admissions of guilt from the other two participants in the chair-pulling incident as well as from the rest of the class. Despite all of this, the little tyke persisted in his adherence to what our depute head, Mr Tod, has taken to calling our new school motto:

'It wisny me, surr,' pleaded McCleary. 'Ah didny dae nuthin'.'

The amorality of modern youth sometimes leaves me speechless.

Tuesday

Simon Young was not in school today; indeed, he will be away for the rest of the week.

'What is it this time?' Mr Pickup asked me at morning break.

'A course on the new Higher, I think,' I told him. 'Either that or a principal teachers' management course.'

'God save us!' remarked Pickup. 'If it's not one thing, it's another. He's hardly been in school since the term started, has he?'

I had to admit that the recent variety of in-service courses which have required Simon's attendance have made his occasional appearances within Parkland High something of a talking point, if not occasions for celebration.

'But he says we'll all benefit from it,' I supported him to Pickup. 'There's going to be a large 'cascade effect' at the end of it all, I understand.'

'Hah!' snorted Pickup. 'The only thing cascading around here is the number of bloody 'please-takes' for us poor sods who're left behind. I've got three this week!'

Pickup's is a very short-sighted view: these courses are clearly vital to the long-term educational interests of our pupils. But then, Pickup has never been able to see beyond the most limited – and selfish – of horizons.

Wednesday

Another departmental absence, this time due to some kind of 'mystery virus'. The missing figure today was Sandra Smart – normally our acting assistant principal, but currently acting PT for Simon Young while away on his residential course.

It meant, of course, that Ian Taylor was temporarily asked to take over the running of the department in addition to his usual guidance responsibilities. Things could be even worse tomorrow when Mr Major departs for a two-day course on 'Time-Management for Assistant Headteachers'.

'Well, Major's absence shouldn't make much difference,' commented Pickup as we prepared ourselves for this evening's school board meeting. 'He's only got four teaching periods in the week anyway, hasn't he?'

'Mmm,' I agreed, '– but three of them are tomorrow.'

Our discussion was cut short by the arrival of Alan Carswell, chairman of the school board, from which position he has already made clear his antipathy to the educational provision which Parkland High makes for his daughter. As some kind of introduction to the meeting, Pickup and I had a little speech lined up to highlight our dissatisfaction with his dictatorial style of chairmanship. For once, we managed to get a word in edgeways before he started, and concluded our plea for greater tolerance and mutual understanding with a thinly veiled threat to withdraw staff representation from the board if a greater degree of co-operation was not forthcoming.

Carswell did not seem unduly worried. 'Good,' he announced curtly. 'Then we might get some work done.'

Speechless again, Pickup and I found ourselves unable to interrupt as Carswell formally opened the meeting. He began with passing reference to the 'dangerous lack of supervision in certain classes' which had come to his attention – this I understood (from the glare aimed in my direction) to be an indirect comment about the practical joke perpetrated on his daughter by McLeary and co. last Monday in my own classroom. I feigned innocence.

Next on the agenda was Mr Carswell's proposed book requisition for the English department. As an alternative to Simon Young's detailed listing of new textbooks (already denounced by him as 'pornographic filth'), he has suggested that we try to open our pupils' minds to the glories of English literature instead of – as he put it – 'allowing them to wallow in the sewers of quasi-literate reading material' which, he insisted, the English department was wont to offer its charges.

Accordingly, a revised list of new textbooks was proposed for purchase: it included, among others, new class sets of *Pilgrim's Progress*, *Jane Eyre* and *Great Expectations*. And that was just for the first year.

I voiced strong opposition, but was drowned out. I don't know what Simon Young will say when he gets back.

Thursday

More rearrangement of departmental responsibilities. Mr Major has been seconded at extremely short notice (an industry liaison course, I understand), so Ian Taylor, as the next most senior teacher available, was asked at even shorter notice to step into his place at the time-management course. It meant that Jan Clark was asked to run the department for the day and – brief moment of glory – I was given the honour of being APT until the end of the week. Pickup, inevitably, had something to say about all of the absences:

'Good grief! Secondments, residential in-service courses, management meetings? I'll tell you something, Morris: what I can't understand is how we ever managed to run a national education system *without* all these courses.'

'Oh, for heaven's sake,' I chided him. 'I've already told you: curricular developments nowadays absolutely *necessitate* the provision of proper in-service training.' Pickup started a derisory comment, but I cut in again. 'And anyway – it gives people like me the chance to have practice at management techniques on a short-term basis.'

'What?' he jumped in. 'You don't mean they've bumped *you* upstairs because of all this?'

Despite his scornful expression, I confirmed my temporary position of assistant principal. Pickup looked worried.

'My God, Morris – a heartbeat away from the presidency, eh? Let's just hope Jan Clark doesn't step under a bus tonight!'

Friday

Pickup's expressions of concern for Jan Clark's welfare yesterday afternoon took a retrospectively ironic twist this morning, when news of her incapacity was telephoned to the school office at 8–50 am. Fortunately, it involved nothing so dramatic as walking under a bus; instead, she appears to have succumbed to the mystery virus affecting the school. Mr Tod looked doleful as he presented me with the news at registration.

'I'm afraid there's nothing else for it, Simpson,' he shook his head sorrowfully. 'With only two members of the actual department present, it looks as if you'll be in charge of English for the day.'

My excitement knew no bounds, though it was tempered with the awesome responsibility of arranging cover of six classes with only four teachers, three of them on a supply basis only. I think I managed to deal with everything, however, as I quietly prided myself at morning break.

'There's really nothing to it,' I told Pickup over a coffee and doughnut. 'Dish out a couple of please-takes, distribute a few sets of books, and you're away. And it should certainly impress the exam board when I apply for a marker's job this summer.'

'You what?' spluttered Pickup into his coffee.

'The exam board. I'm applying for a marker's post this year. I'd think that short-term experience of running a department will make them keen to have me.'

'Yes, yes, I'm sure they *will* be keen to have you. But what on earth are you *doing* it for?'

'Well, the money, mainly. I'm hoping to go abroad this year, and I thought I'd be able to supplement my income with –'

Pickup exploded with laughter as the bell interrupted our conversation, but he still found time to place an avuncular hand on my shoulder and advise me not to plan any expensive trips on the proceeds of my SCE marking. He claimed it was the one area of worker exploitation which the Factory Acts seem to have passed by . . .

Unfortunately, I had no time to take the matter further later on, because my day became peculiarly chaotic after the interval. In retrospect I can see where I went wrong, but it was some thirty minutes into the period before it became apparent that I had sent three supply teachers to the same classroom, whilst leaving two other groups devoid of any supervision whatsoever.

Of course, I had to leave 1P unsupervised while I tried to sort it all out, and it was some twenty minutes before I could return to restore order. Tommy McShane and Alan McLeary, needless to say, were involved in a large-scale re-enactment of a football riot. And Janie Carswell, for her part, seemed intent upon checking her watch every time I entered and left the room, after which she would make brief notes in a jotter at the side of her desk. She refused to let me see the contents when I asked, remarking that the jotter was private property belonging to her father.

At least, I thought, I would be able to sort out McLeary and McShane with my comments on their respective conduct cards at the end of the period. I made great show of ticking the lowest available grades again, but was saddened to witness their return to my door, accompanied by Mr Tod, some twenty minutes after lunch.

'These boys have been wandering round the school since lunchtime, Mr Simpson,' he informed me coldly, brandishing their conduct cards aloft. 'And I gather it's on your instructions?'

I denied all knowledge, until Tod reminded me that my comments on their conduct cards had involved an immediate referral to my principal teacher who, on this occasion, happened to be acting in a temporary capacity.

'You bone-head, Simpson,' he hissed audibly, much to the amusement of McLeary and McShane, '– you've referred them to *yourself*!'

Horrified, I confessed responsibility and promised to take the matter in hand at once – or at least as soon as I'd finished arranging cover for the rest of the department.

I don't think I'll mention being a principal teacher to the exam board.

March

Mr Pickup was perfectly correct in his assertion that very few teachers who involve themselves in marking SCE (Scottish Certificate of Education) examination scripts do so in order to supplement their income. If this is their aim, they would be better off serving in a pub.

Payment rates, and speed of marking, will mean that different applicants might enjoy slightly different rewards for their time and labours, but the starting point for payment is comparatively low in the first place, and even the swiftest marker can only aim at an hourly rate which would make refuse-collection an enviable source of alternative employment. Indeed, the two jobs could be said to have much in common . . .

However, a regular appointment as a marker for the SEB (Scottish Examination Board) does indeed allow a teacher to keep more closely in touch with the requirements for examinations, and the associated chances of advancement within the profession are a considerable draw to a teacher like Morris Simpson, intent – as ever – upon making a name for himself.

However, his March diary reveals that a new obsession was about to enter Morris's life. As a student teacher, Fiona Strangelove was more precocious – and more attractive – than most. The familiar ease with which she ventured into the blackboard jungle of Parkland High led to expressions of professional jealousy from more than a few members of staff, Mr Pickup included. And her wanton disregard for staffroom protocol led to feelings of mistrust and annoyance from the older members of staff such as Mr Major. But for Morris, there was only one word to express the emotion he felt towards Fiona Strangelove.

Lust.

Monday

A student arrived in the department this morning. Miss Strangelove is a strikingly attractive blonde in an extremely short skirt who took very little time to make herself at home. In point of fact, she alienated herself from our assistant headteacher, Mr Major, immediately upon arrival in the staffroom at morning break: she seated herself in his cherished corner armchair and ignored all his pointed remarks that she should consider removing herself.

'Oh, come off it,' she smiled coyly up at him. 'The chairs are for *everybody* in the staffroom, aren't they?' Adding insult to injury, she took a sip of coffee from the mug to which she'd lain claim, a mug which bore the legend **R. MAJOR – PERSONAL PROPERTY** painted boldly on its side. Major pursed his lips, lit a pipe and retired, china cup in hand, to perch upon a tall stool next to the door – a position in which he looked most uncomfortable, to say the least. I almost felt sorry for the man.

I nevertheless decided to extend the hand of friendship to the young girl and introduced myself as a member of the school board, as well as of the English department with which she would be spending most of her time.

'Actually,' I confided in a vain attempt to impress her further, 'I was acting principal teacher quite recently, but I'm back in the infantry now.'

She certainly seemed interested. 'How long were you acting up, then?' she enquired.

'Well, just the one day, actually – but it was very good experience. If I can offer you any help . . . er . . . ?' I enquired.

'Fiona,' she answered. 'Thanks. But why just the one day?'

I decided not to acquaint her with the embarrassing details of my brief moment of power at the helm of the department last month. Instead, I turned the conversation round to her teaching experience so far, and asked if she still felt nervous in front of a class.

'Nervous?' she laughed. 'Why should I? I love it. And the kids are just *great*!'

She seems a striking and extremely confident young lady, as I remarked to Mr Pickup at lunchtime; however, he was inclined to disagree.

'Cocky little bitch,' he adjudged. 'Give her 1P tomorrow and see how she copes!'

Maybe I will.

Tuesday

Pickup's suggestion has backfired slightly. I followed his suggestion of throwing Fiona Strangelove in at the deep end by presenting her with the school's most unruly class of ruffians, but she had them eating out of her hand after five minutes. I sneaked a look through the door panel after another quarter of an hour to check that Tommy McShane hadn't actually killed anyone yet – it seemed awfully quiet – and there she was, sitting atop my desk, legs provocatively crossed, calmly reading poetry to them!

I congratulated her in the staffroom afterwards.

'Why?' she asked me. 'It wasn't anything special – they seem a nice bunch of kids, and as soon as I'd turfed out that theme study that someone had dreamt up for them, we got on like a house on fire.'

I chose to conceal my authorship of the theme study she had elected to discard so carelessly, and asked her instead how she was getting on at college.

'Oh, great,' she enthused, '– but there's nothing to beat actually coming into schools and getting down to real *teaching* with real *kids* . . .'

Pickup, listening in the background, gave an enormous and ill-concealed snort of derision, and retired behind the pages of his newspaper.

Fiona seemed not to notice. 'But they'd be horrified in college,' she continued, 'to see some of the rooms here.'

'How d'you mean?' I asked.

'Well, yours is all right, Morris,' she smiled at me, 'but that one next to you, for example – it must be a right old fogey's class. The desks are all in straight rows, and there's hardly a picture on the wall or a book to be seen anywhere. How on earth d'you get on with pupil-centred, resource-based learning in an atmosphere like that?'

Pickup emerged from behind his newspaper. 'You don't!' he snarled. 'And I'd thank you to keep your fancy college notions to yourself, young lady. It's *my* room and I'll arrange it how I like!'

Fiona flushed ever so slightly, bit her lip, and looked downwards. She really is a most attractive girl.

Wednesday

Class 1P were in near-revolt this morning when they discovered Miss Strangelove would not be taking them for English.

'Aw, surr,' complained Alan McLeary. 'That's no' ferr! She wis magic, so she wis.'

Typical. I beat my brains out for a year trying to educate and entertain them, and a new face – albeit an extremely pretty one – comes along to take all the glory. I was saying as much to Pickup before the school board meeting tonight, and he chose to deliver a timely warning:

'Just watch yourself, Simpson,' he chided. 'The way you've been looking at that young female, it's not only 1P that thinks she's a bit of all right. Keep clear, sonny – she'd eat you for breakfast.'

To be honest, there was a degree of truth in Pickup's assessment of my feelings towards Miss Strangelove, but I think he's totally misguided in his appraisal of her – I'm pretty sure she feels a certain respect for an experienced teacher like myself.

My thoughts on the matter meant I was unable to pay full attention to the board proceedings, and it was probably just as well. Mr Carswell, the chairman, spent most of the evening berating the recent appearance of 'graphic advertisements for teenage prophylactics all over the school'. Mr Pickup tried, in vain, to explain that the large posters and publicity materials for condoms which have recently appeared in senior cloakrooms and common rooms were part of a health education course designed to alert young people to the dangers of unprotected sexual activity. It cut no ice.

'Bollocks!' Carswell replied. 'It's just encouraging the lot of them to indulge in pre-marital sex, and I'm not having it! Get those posters down by the end of the week, or I'll have the local press on to this one!'

Mindful of our last encounter with the *Parkland Gazette*, Pickup sighed and said he would see the guidance staff tomorrow. I think I'll resign from the school board at the end of the session.

Thursday

Have decided to ask Miss Strangelove out for a date. I tried to make the suggestion at morning break and lunchtime, but on both occasions discovered I lacked the nerve at the last minute.

I decided to try again at afternoon break, by telling her that I'd been selected to act as a marker for Higher English this year, after which I planned to ask her if she'd like to join me for a celebratory meal. However, she seemed singularly unimpressed by my selection as a marker:

'Really?' she curled an attractive and disbelieving upper lip. '– they picked *you* . . . ?'

My courage collapsed.

Friday

Still no joy with Miss Strangelove – rather the opposite, in fact. Having offered her the opportunity to take my fourth year class this afternoon, I was distressed to learn that she had been forced to witness one of the most disgusting examples of pupil misbehaviour which I've come across in all my teaching career.

It started when she entered the staffroom some ten minutes into the lesson. I had taken the opportunity to catch up on some marking, much to Pickup's amusement, when Miss Strangelove – white-faced and obviously shaken – asked for my presence in the classroom.

'One of the boys has been very, very sick, Morris – and I don't think it's something he's eaten . . .'

Puzzled, I followed her out to Hut A57 to discover the distressing sight of big George Crawford spreadeagled across his desk, a soporific grin on his face and lying, to my horror, in a large pool of vomit which had spread across the folder of work on his desk and was slowly dripping to the varnished floor beneath. A strong smell of whisky surrounded the sleeping wretch. Most of the class were understandably unhappy about the prevailing stench, so I cleared the room of all pupils except Crawford before trying to rouse him from his glutinous slumbers.

Mr Tod had arrived on the scene by now and, between us, we managed to haul Crawford to the depute's room for an explanation of his appalling behaviour, as related to me later by Tod. It seemed that one of the boy's cronies had raided the parental drinks cabinet the night before and had brought in several large 'cocktail bottles' of assorted beers and spirits for a Friday lunchtime drinking session. Crawford, alas, found himself overcome by the effects of a quarter bottle of raw spirit with the consequences already presented to me by Fiona Strangelove.

To be honest, I wasn't really interested in the origins of the affair by four o'clock. My mind just kept going back to the appalling insensitivity which I'd displayed to Fiona in helping her clear up the mess left by Crawford's classroom regurgitation. I failed to endear myself to her when she handed me a rather soggy folder, held distastefully between thumb and forefinger: 'Well, Fiona,' I smiled, trying to make light of the whole affair, '– this is what teaching's all about, y'know. How d'you fancy trying to assess *this* for a Standard grade folio?'

She wasn't amused, so I tried to redeem the situation. 'Umm . . . sorry,' I apologised. Trying desperately to think of some avenue for conversation, some opening for my invitation, I eventually launched myself – unawares and regardless – with what was, in that particular context, an inopportune suggestion: 'Look,' I declared brightly. 'How d'you fancy joining me for a Chinese meal tonight?'

With hindsight, I can understand her distress. She took one look at the dripping folder, the soiled desk and vomit-strewn floor, then asked me angrily if I thought I was being funny suggesting Chinese meals – and scurried off in the direction of the ladies' toilets, a handkerchief pressed against her mouth.

'Does that mean you're not coming?' I quavered uselessly after her. It did.

Strangely enough, I found her even more attractive when she was angry like that. I shall bide my time and make another approach.

April

It was spring, and Morris Simpson was intent upon enjoying the excitement of new life which was blossoming all around him. Romance can make an enormous difference in a young man's life, and Morris was no exception: a few short months ago he had been careworn, depressed and preoccupied with a multitude of educational concerns. Now life seemed different, and it was Fiona Strangelove he had to thank for the new-found confidence in his step, the newly-discovered awareness of nature's bountiful harvest.

Life was not so grand for others. Senior school pupils, for example, had the traumatic onset of Standard and Higher grade examinations, always awkwardly timetabled for the hottest, stickiest time of year when the attractions of studying indoors compare most unfavourably with the prospect of a refreshing walk in the great outdoors. Ultimately, of course, Morris would have to turn his attentions towards marking the scripts from their examinations, to be sat during the last week of April. He looked forward with keen anticipation to his first ever markers' meeting.

Another person for whom life had proved frustrating of late was Monica Cunningham, Parkland's principal teacher of computing. Her complaints about the fabric of her department were not new: indeed, she had spent most of her non-contact time since August in trying to persuade the regional authorities to repair the poorly maintained electrical sockets with which she was forced to work. Additionally, she had been infuriated by the appalling security for some of the exorbitantly expensive equipment which her department contained.

Morris, aglow with altruistic affection for all, pondered long and hard over Mrs Cunningham's problems. As he understood it, there was a newly appointed DEO (divisional education officer) at the regional offices, and he was a man who knew what he was about. His diary for April takes up the story.

Monday

A flurry of complaints at morning interval from Monica Cunningham, principal teacher of computing, about the state of her department.

'Honestly!' she launched a coffee-table monologue in the direction of anyone prepared to listen, '– it's a disgrace! There are still no proper security locks on the doors, and half of the electrical points aren't working properly.'

I nodded sympathetically – my own classroom in Hut A57 has experienced similar problems. I started to tell her about it, but she was in full flight:

'And not only that: the electrical points that *are* working are positively unsafe – there's a running *stream* of water which comes down one of the inside walls: it's only a matter of time before someone's electrocuted. I've asked the janitor to do something about it till I'm blue in the face – I think I'm going to take it up with the clerk of works instead!'

'Hmm,' I mused, mindful of my own experience with the regional works authority some two and a half years ago now. I decided to offer wiser counsel instead: 'I don't think I'd waste my time on him, Monica. Why don't you try writing to Mr Baxter instead?'

'What? The new education officer? Surely it's not his remit?'

'Not really. But it means you're going straight to the top, and Dan Baxter's got a very strong reputation for getting things done – I think he might get swifter action for you. Maybe get yourself noticed by him, too . . .'

Monica furrowed a brow in reflection, then clearly decided to follow my advice: 'Yes, Morris,' she smiled gratefully as she turned to leave: '– maybe I will get in touch with Dan Baxter. Thanks for the suggestion.'

It was nice to be able to help her, I thought to myself. If only my own problems were so easily solved; alas, however, I continue to suffer the pangs of unrequited love.

To explain, Fiona Strangelove is the devastatingly attractive blonde student who's been assigned to our department for the summer term, and whom I've already failed to impress to any great extent. Unfortunately, she spent much of her free time today in earnest conversation with Frank Parker, our temporary APT guidance from the physics department, so I had little time to further my chances. Maybe tomorrow.

Tuesday

No luck with Fiona. I tried to draw her admiration at morning interval again, this time by dropping into the conversation the fact that I wouldn't be here on Friday because of my markers' meeting for the Higher grade examination. She curled her upper lip in obvious disappointment, and my heart leapt, but it soon became apparent that her distress was not due to my impending absence.

'Sorry, Frank,' she turned to Mr Parker. 'I won't make it along to your guidance tutorial on Friday after all – looks like I'll have to take Mr Simpson's class instead.'

'Morris,' I corrected her gently, laying a gentle hand on her shoulder. 'Please call me Morris.'

She looked down with obvious distaste at the position of my hand and turned deliberately away, before embarking upon another intense conversation with Frank Parker.

Maybe she's just playing hard to get . . .

Wednesday

Monica Cunningham's letter to the divisional education officer has been rewarded with instant results, though not in the manner which she had expected.

Apparently, she sent off a fiery epistle in the direction of the regional offices, urging Mr Baxter to make it his utmost priority to do something about the dangerous conditions and inadequate security facilities for Parkland High School's computers. It was, she had pointed out in her letter, a poor reflection upon divisional standards that her pupils had to work in such conditions; furthermore, as she later told us, she had refused to be held responsible should any computing equipment be stolen as a result of faulty security provision.

It was a threat too far, apparently: Mr Baxter's reputation for swift action was confirmed when she arrived in her classroom this morning to discover that he had ordered the immediate removal from the premises of her entire computer stock.

'But he can't do that!' she shouted at Mrs Thomson in the school office at ten past nine.

'Well, he did,' replied Mrs Thomson, angrily handing Monica the goods retrieval form signed by Mr Baxter and presented to the office staff some 30 minutes previous by a van driver who had emptied the computer room in double-quick time. Apparently alarmed by the possible consequences described in Monica's letter, our new DEO had decided that the best course of action was to remove the possible source of controversy altogether, and – much to Monica's distress – redistribute the items throughout other schools in the region.

Needless to say, Monica Cunningham took it out on me in front of the whole staffroom – including Fiona Strangelove – at morning break:

'Thanks for the advice, Morris,' she ladled a heavy dose of sarcasm across the coffee counter. 'Got any bright ideas about teaching computing without any computers?'

I parried as best I could – the woman was in no mood for rational argument – and went instead to look for a quiet corner and some solace from Mr Pickup. I needn't have bothered.

He proceeded to tell me, in no uncertain detail, that he could have warned me about the new DEO's reaction from the start: he had apparently been at teacher training college with 'Dangerous Dan Baxter', as he persisted in calling him, and knew him of old. 'He's a hard-man, Simpson – and he doesn't take crap from wee wifies like Monica Cunningham – or from anyone else, come to that.'

I told him he was being wise after the event, as usual, so he launched another attack.

'Not always *after* the event, young fellow; sometimes before it, as well,' he leaned back into his armchair and looked archly across the room at Fiona Strangelove.

'Pardon?' I bristled, 'What d'you mean by that?'

'That young woman over there. She may still have you dangling on a string, but in your place I'd forget it. She and Frank Parker look ready to seal the knot at any time from where I'm siting.'

'What?' I glanced sharply across the room. 'Don't be ridiculous, Pickup. They've only known each other for five weeks. And anyway, Fiona's already told me about Frank – she's just interested in guidance, that's all, and Frank's been giving her one or two pointers, letting her sit in on a few tutorials.'

'Haw!' Pickup guffawed rudely. 'Don't give me that! The only tutorials Frank Parker's likely to give are in the finer points of boudoir athletics, and if you think –'

I interrupted at once and told him I didn't wish to hear any more. Fiona's not that type of girl.

Thursday

One in the eye for Pickup. I got Fiona to relent and agree to meet me for a drink sometime. She must have forgotten about my markers' meeting, because she suggested four o'clock after school tomorrow. I tried three alternative dates and times, but Friday appeared to be the only one that suited her.

'O.K.,' I finally agreed. 'Four o'clock tomorrow, then.'

She seemed slightly taken aback. 'But haven't you got a markers' meeting for the Higher literature paper?' she queried – rather too hopefully, I couldn't help thinking.

'Oh, that's all right,' I assured her. 'I'll get a bus back in time, don't worry. See you then?'

'Um . . .' She seemed uncertain, but eventually agreed: 'Oh . . . all right. If you must.'

It was hardly the most romantic of acceptances, but at least it's a start.

Friday

My first markers' meeting – and what an eye-opener.

I made a bad start by arriving fifteen minutes late. 'Sorry,' I apologised to Mr Harvey, the principal examiner, as I blundered across the room in search of an empty seat. 'Took me longer than I expected getting here . . .'

He coughed gently and carried on once I'd settled down.

Most of the morning was taken up with marking, in groups, some sample scripts which had been selected from those already received. As a first time marker, I was assigned to a group with Mr Harvey in charge and, along with the other members, I was given six different essays to assess.

Having settled down to give each one the care and attention I thought necessary, I was just coming to the end of my second reading of Answer One when Mr Harvey announced 'Time Up' and requested our respective verdicts on each of the six essays.

I looked up in surprise. 'But I haven't even finished Answer One yet,' I protested. 'You can't just –'

'Sorry, Mr . . . eh . . . ?'

'Simpson. Morris Simpson,' I informed him.

'Yes. Sorry, Mr Simpson, but you have to get a move on in this business, y'know. Otherwise you'll still be marking your scripts come Christmas Day.'

'But –'

'Anyway,' he interrupted me again. 'If you've done Answer One, we'll start with that one. What did you give it?'

'Well, I haven't actually finished yet, but I was thinking of around ten or eleven out of twenty.'

'Oh yes?' he looked doubtfully at me. 'Why?'

'Well, I suppose it has to pass – the candidate *does* seem to have a decent appreciation of the poem, but really, the essay's so full of poor spelling and contorted syntax that it's almost unintelligible at times. And another thing –'

'Anyone else have comments?' Mr Harvey interrupted me once more – rather sharply, I thought.

The ensuing ten minutes proved rather embarrassing. Nobody seemed to agree with my assessment, including Mr Harvey: they all appeared to think that the creative and appreciative merits of the essay outweighed anything so minor as its disgraceful spelling and sentence construction. An eventual mark of seventeen out of twenty was agreed upon. I was appalled.

And so it went on. When I thought an essay worthy of praise, it usually meant a failure mark from everyone else, frequently on the basis that it didn't seem to be a 'genuinely personal response', whatever that may be. If I saw fit to fail an essay, others found themselves arguing whether it should be a 'low A grade' or a 'high B'. The day left me drained and apprehensive about the coming weeks, when I would start marking the damned things for real.

I mentioned my concerns to Mr Harvey at the end of the afternoon, and he told me not to worry – he would be keeping a special eye on my scripts, anyway.

I wasn't sure whether that was a good thing or not, but put the whole affair out of my mind as I rushed to catch the bus for my date with Fiona.

Alas, the bus was late, and it was touch and go as to whether it would reach Parkland in time for four o'clock. Unfortunately, it lumbered around the corner leading to the school entrance at five minutes past the hour. I alighted, and was just in time to witness Fiona and Frank Parker walking hand in hand out of the school and towards Frank's car, a Cavalier GTi. They stopped and, to my horror, kissed each other affectionately before getting into their respective seats. More kissing – and fondling, as far as I could see – ensued as Frank started the engine; then, with a roar of exhaust fumes and a screeching of tyres, they roared out of the school gates, Fiona laying an affectionate head on her chauffeur's shoulder.

I shrank into the bus shelter, and hoped they hadn't seen me. The next bus home wasn't for another half hour.

I decided to walk instead.

May

As Morris was attending his first markers' meeting, another educational innovation was being launched from an office elsewhere in Scotland. Bill Thomson, an adviser in modern languages, was putting the finishing touches to his requests for pilot schools in the primary modern languages project.

In a laudable venture aimed at enlarging European awareness, a limited number of secondary schools – plus their associated primaries – were to be accorded pilot status in a programme aimed at 'starting them young' in the business of learning foreign languages. It was ironic that one of the schools which received the invitation to join in the scheme was Parkland Community High: when the letters were received at the end of May, it became clear – from his unhappy reaction – that Jack Ferguson was *not* one of the scheme's more enthusiastic supporters.

Yet if Jack Ferguson was unhappy, Morris Simpson could be more accurately described as devastated. As if it wasn't enough to be losing the battle for the affections of Fiona Strangelove, he was also lumbered with the most appalling backlog of marking which had accumulated since his very first day of starting the Higher marking. There just seemed to be so *many* of the damned scripts, and the longer he stayed up each night to deal with them, the more exhausted he became. And so it went on . . .

Monday

My attempts to keep up with the Higher marking fall further and further behind. I even slept in this morning as a result of an 'all night sitting' yesterday evening, which saw me eventually retire to bed around 3 am. Mr Tod, our irascible depute, was not pleased to welcome my bleary-eyed presence to the school at twenty past nine, and spent some time berating me over my lack of punctuality. Frankly, it was all I could do to stop myself yawning into his face.

Consequently, I was in no mood to listen to Jack Ferguson's vitriolic atack on his modern lanuages adviser at morning break, but – so voluble were his complaints – I had little choice.

'Good God almighty!' he unfolded a letter which he had withdrawn from his pigeon-hole. 'That's all I need!'

'What's up, Jack?' asked Mr Pickup. 'Still not granted you your early retirement, then?'

'Worse than that,' scowled Ferguson in reply. 'They're trying to give me *more* work to do. This damned primary languages project – Bill Thomson's wanting me to organise a taster course for Primary 7 down the road,' he gestured in the general direction of Parkland Primary, our local feeder school. 'And that's only the start,' he read on angrily: 'Next year he wants a full integration of our languages timetable with theirs, and a permanent weekly secondment of two of our staff members to go and drum some French into the little darlings before they reach the exalted heights of secondary school. What a bloody waste of time,' he shook his head sadly. 'As if they hadn't tried all this twenty years ago, and we all know what happened when it –'

'Oh, I dunno, Jack,' interrupted Pickup. 'Look on the bright side: could be a chance to get out of this dump for a couple of afternoons a week. And just think of the travelling expenses . . .'

Mr Ferguson did not seem convinced, but I was unable to keep awake long enough to follow the rest of the conversation. My head must have drooped, for the next thing I felt was Mr Tod shaking me violently by the shoulder and asking if I didn't have a class to go to? I did.

Tuesday

I am still unable to win the affection of Fiona Strangelove, the devastatingly attractive blonde student who has been placed with the English department this term. I thought I'd cracked it this morning when I taught a lesson to 2F with Fiona observing from the back of the class. It was, in all modesty, a fairly impressive performance on my part, which I felt sure would make a good impression on her.

Alas, she rejected my suggestion afterwards that we spend half an hour discussing the aims and objectives of the lesson; instead, she pleaded a previous engagement with Frank Parker, my colleague from guidance and physics, whose company she so obviously values above the furtherance of her educational career.

Actually, her refusal – though emotionally wounding – nevertheless allowed me to try and catch up on some Higher marking. Contrary to all regulations, I had smuggled a bundle of papers into school to catch up on the enormous backlog I seem to have generated. Having just started our new timetable, I had no first year classes, so locked the door of my room at lunchtime and settled down to an afternoon's sustained assessment, free of the distractions of any children.

Foolishly, I wasted a good deal of time in trying to devise an accelerated timetable of marking: having worked out that I was currently getting through three scripts in every hour, I eventually realised that I would need to improve this to seven scripts per hour if my deadline were to be met; unfortunately, the counting of scripts and mathematical calculations involved in arriving at this conclusion used up a further thirty-five minutes, which delay threw me even further behind schedule.

Cast into depression, I managed a further two scripts before finding myself overcome with yet more drowsiness. Drastically, I appear to have fallen into a deep, deep sleep, from which I could only be roused by the combined knockings on the door at 4 o'clock of my cleaner, Mrs Young, demanding entrance, and Mr Pickup, who wanted to know if I 'fancied a quick pint'.

Against my better judgement, I accepted Pickup's invitation, on the sole condition that it *was* a quick one and that I would leave for home as soon as possible to catch up with the marking. It was a forlorn hope.

Wednesday

A fearsome panic over my Higher scripts. In my hasty departure from school last night, I appear to have left two envelopes among the accumulated débris on my desk. Mrs Young, in one of her more enthusiastic moods, chose last night of all nights to launch a comprehensive cleansing offensive, and swept the majority of the desk's contents into a large black bin bag – examination scripts included!

I spent an embarrassing twenty minutes searching the bins outside the kitchens before locating the offending papers, and a further fifteen cleaning the remnants of fish-heads and kitchen slops from around their edges. I hope nobody at the exam board notices.

The entire episode caused Pickup much amusement, and he lost no time in re-telling it to the assembled staffroom company at lunchtime. He soon had the smile wiped off his face, however, when he moved on to tell Jack Ferguson that he needn't worry any more about the primary languages project. As union representative, he informed Ferguson that all co-operation in the scheme was to be withdrawn until the fuller educational and financial implications had been approved by the union's executive council.

'So you needn't go after all, Jacko,' Pickup smiled. 'In fact – you can't: as union representative, I'd forbid your involvement! How does that suit you?'

Mr Ferguson pondered a moment, then took the wind out of Pickup's sails completely. 'It doesn't, Pickup. Doesn't suit me at all.'

'You what? But I thought you said –'

'Well, maybe I did,' Ferguson cut in. 'But I've been thinking, and the prospect of leaving a grotty fourth year to somebody else in the department while I nip off for a class of twenty-one eager eleven-year olds has a good deal of attraction. And then there are the travelling expenses, as you so rightly –'

'But you can't,' interrupted Pickup. 'It's not union policy. We don't approve, and it's –'

'And the final thing which made up my mind for me,' Ferguson cut in icily, 'was your ridiculous assertion that any union could tell *me* what to do. I'm a grown man, Pickup, and I'll make up my *own* mind about how I approach curricular innovations such as this.'

There was a certain irony in Ferguson's remarks, given the complete U-Turn which he had just accomplished over the issue, and especially given the fact that the most recent curricular innovation with which he had been involved would probably have been the arrival of overhead projectors into his classroom some twenty years ago.

Nevertheless, he stood firm, despite Pickup's attempts to persuade him otherwise: for once, it looks as if Parkland High will be in the forefront of educational reform – with, it must be added, a somewhat unlikely vanguard in the person of Jack Ferguson.

Thursday

Mr Ferguson departed for Parkland Primary this afternoon, full of touching expectation and with an enormous yellow folder under his arm, inscribed 'PRIMARY LIAISON' on the side in large black felt pen.

'Ach,' muttered Pickup as he watched him leave – 'it's full of colouring-in pencils, that's all. What d'you think, Morris . . . ?'

I had little inclination to discuss the matter with him, for I was still smarting from a final showdown with Fiona Strangelove. The young madam had chosen to reject my suggestion that we spend some time this afternoon devising an oral assessment package after school.

'Look, Morris,' she had responded bluntly. 'Why don't you bog off? In case you hadn't noticed, Frank Parker and I are getting on really well together and, quite frankly, I'd have to be pretty desperate to spend an evening – or even an afternoon – alone with you. Once and for all, it's no go. D'you understand that?'

As a knock-back, it was fairly comprehensive. I have promised not to bother her again, and have instead promised myself to channel all such energies into completing my Higher marking as soon as possible. As sublimation goes, I can think of better alternatives, but at least it'll keep me busy.

Alas, my good intentions suffered an early setback this afternoon: having just settled down for some staffroom marking, I was diverted by a leaflet on teacher placement schemes which had been left in my pigeon-hole. It looks a fairly interesting prospect, whereby teachers can get involved with the real world of work through a series of

71

industrial placements, and I found myself intrigued by the possibility of applying.

'What d'you think?' I asked Mr Pickup, waving the leaflet across his newspaper. 'Perhaps I could go on one of these during the holidays? It might be a good opening for promotion, if nothing else, and it says you get a real sense of curricular enrichment by going through with it.'

Pickup was rather dismissive of the proposal, as I might have expected. Instead, he plans to spend two weeks of his summer break with a group of fifth and sixth year pupils on a beach holiday in Italy, which, he says, will give him all the curricular enrichment he needs.

I told him I thought it was hardly very educational, but he seemed unconcerned by my opinion, as usual. I think I'll apply for one of these placements, anyway: I've always fancied being a captain of industry . . .

Friday

Mr Ferguson's hopes for an easier primary lifestyle appear to have been dashed.

He arrived in the staffroom at lunchtime, straight from his morning session with Primary 7b down the road. He looked older: much, much older.

'Little bastards!' he gritted through clenched teeth. 'Absolute little bastards!' And so saying, he flung his carefully inscribed folder to the corner, where it remained throughout the afternoon.

Further investigation revealed that a surprisingly substantial number of disciplinary problems had arisen with his young charges. He was unwilling to outline events in any great detail, but it became clear that Parkland Primary's insistence on group methods of working had been alien to all of Mr Ferguson's teaching experience to date. Furthermore, he had been unable to accommodate the more relaxed attitute towards levels of working noise in the average primary classroom today:

'The little buggers wouldn't shut up!' he swore angrily. 'There I am, trying to explain to one group how they should ask for a railway ticket to Lyons, and all the time the others are prattling on to each other about what they've just been told to do instead of getting on and doing it! I bawl my head off to no avail, and then their own teacher – *their own teacher, mark you* – backs them up, tells me it's an indication of their interest in the subject. Tells me I've got to be able to differentiate between an unproductive noise and a workman-like buzz, so help me!'

And on he went. Infuriated beyond belief at receiving unwanted professional advice from a young lady some twenty-six years his junior – 'the wee bint was still in her pram when *I* started teaching,' Ferguson correctly pointed out – he had declared his pilot programme of primary liaison closed for the time being and had left early at lunchtime.

'And if they want me back,' he growled, 'they can get their desks into straight rows for a start. If they think –'

I left the staffroom as he launched into another assault on primary school methodology. It was time for me to telephone Mr Harvey, the chief examiner in English. Having found myself still unable to complete my allocation of scripts in time, I had decided to lay my cards on the table.

It took some time to get through to the exam board, for Mr Harvey seemed to be in a meeting of some kind. I assured the telephonist that it was urgent, however, and she went to get him.

'Ah, hullo, Mr Harvey,' I began brightly. 'Morris Simpson here, Parkland High: look, it's about these Higher literature scripts I'm supposed to be marking.'

'Yes . . . ?' he growled ominously down the line.

'Yes. Look, I'm afraid there's just no way that I'm going to get them to you in time. I've got far too –'

'Mr Simpson,' he interrupted me. 'The late delivery of scripts is not an option which is open to you. There is a date by which they are due to be received here, and that date, I need hardly remind you, is getting closer. They had better be here by then: that is all I have to say on the matter, except that I am in the middle of a very important meeting – excuse me. Goodbye . . .'

The line went dead. He was hardly what I would call helpful.

I scurried back to the staffroom to collect my scripts. It looked like being a long weekend.

73

June

The examination scripts were, eventually, completed in time for Mr Harvey's deadline, although Morris would be the first to admit that – especially in some of the later batches – he had sacrificed accuracy in marking for expediency of returns. Suffice to say that six minutes per script became the necessary deadline, as opposed to the average of 45 careful minutes which he had devoted to each candidate at the very beginning of his awesome task.

He anticipated the long summer break with relish, as did Sandra Denver, freshly returned from maternity leave just in time to take up her full post before the holidays began. For Morris, of course, the main excitement of his holiday period would be his industrial placement, which he viewed as a welcome (and career-enhancing) break from routine. It had been a difficult session, what with the various measures of unpleasantness over the school board, not to mention his unrequited passion for Fiona Strangelove. And yet, as the final spasm of the term approached, he realised that forgetting both of these issues might be no easy task. And he was *still* awaiting his due financial reward for the Herculean efforts with the exam scripts – as his June diary explains.

Monday

The last week of term, and I am still waiting for payment from the Scottish Examination Board in recompense for my marking activities last month. It is now nearly four weeks since I posted my final envelope of scripts – after all the effort I put into getting the damned things completed on time, you'd think the least they could do would be to arrange for prompt payment. It's all most annoying – I shall need the extra cash quite soon to finance my industrial placement next month.

I've spent some time leafing through the brochure of available placements, and have eventually come to the conclusion that I would like to try my hand at hotel management: I have a feeling that there might be more of a future in the leisure industry than in education, besides which it should give me a chance to develop my interpersonal communication skills to a greater degree – and that should certainly look impressive on my next application for a promoted post!

Tuesday

Great news! Frank Parker and Fiona Strangelove – the attractive blonde student who was with the English department this term – have split up. Mr Pickup passed the joyous tidings to me at morning break.

'Yup,' he declared in explanation of Parker's gloomy staffroom countenance. 'Within a week of getting back to teacher-training college, Fiona had been to three end-of-term discos and started four extra relationships – two of them with hulking great beanbaggers.'

'Beanbaggers?' queried Bob Major, listening in.

'P.E. students,' Pickup explained. 'A couple of one-night stands with each of them, apparently, and the next thing we know is that Frank's got the old heave-ho. Probably just as well, actually,' he mused,' – I think she was wearing him out, by the look of his morning appearances recently. Some girl, our Fiona . . .'

I wasn't really listening any more, or I would have taken him to task over the dubious references to Fiona's moral integrity. All I could think of was the fact that Frank's departure from her life meant that she might be more amenable to further approaches from my good self. The problem of how to get in touch with her again was solved almost immediately as I latched once more on to Pickup's continuing monologue:

'What was that?' I asked him. 'What did you say just then?'

'I said it could be pretty awkward if she *does* come back next session, couldn't it?'

'Who? Fiona?'

'No – the Princess of ruddy Wales!'

'Sorry?'

'Yes, of course Fiona! She's planning to apply for a job here, I understand. Quite close for travelling, and she claims she had a lot of fun here. Wants to –'

I stopped listening again, unable to believe my luck. Imagine: a chance to work full-time with one of the most attractive looking women ever to step through the doors of Parkland High. I hope she gets the job – I can't help wondering if her application's got something to do with the help I gave her in making up lesson-plans this term; and I certainly hope she remembers it come August . . .

Wednesday

Prizegiving Day. This was originally scheduled for Friday, but was moved to Wednesday in consideration of the likely attendance figures for the last day of term. Mr Ross is understandably unwilling to offer a rectorial invitation to assorted councillors and local dignitaries for an occasion when the staff would probably outnumber the pupils on view.

The day passed off well enough with the exception of a minor altercation between myself and Alan Carswell, chairman of the school board, at the sherry reception afterwards.

'Well, Mr Simpson,' jibed Carswell. 'Looking forward to your long holidays, eh?'

I made polite assent and refused to rise to the bait; however, he had the bit between his teeth, and would not let the matter rest. 'Six weeks, eh?' he questioned me. 'Not to mention the endless round of public holidays you've just had this term. Can't be bad now, can it, Mr Simpson? Wish *I* could afford to take holidays as long as that . . .'

Gently, I tried to point out that the stressful implications of a teacher's job today necessitated a reasonable period of summer recuperation but he suggested, rather rudely and with complete inaccuracy, that I did not know the meaning of the word 'stress'.

I was furious, but controlled myself enough to divert the conversation by telling him that I, for my part, would not be entirely on holiday anyway.

'Oh?' he enquired archly. 'What are you doing, then? Spot of teaching to an empty classroom? Could solve the disciline problems, eh, Mr Simpson?'

As politely as I could, I informed him of the industrial placement which I am to undertake, and outlined the curricular enrichment which I am likely to experience as a result of my two weeks learning about management techniques in the leisure industry.

He snorted in derision, so I decided to close the conversation without further ado. 'I'll tell you all about it at the next school board meeting, Mr Carswell. I'll look forward to seeing you then,' I lied blatantly, and scurried off in search of another sherry while the headmaster wasn't looking.

Imagine him saying that teachers don't know the meaning of stress. What a cheek! He should try doing the job himself!

Thursday

Hardly any pupils in school today, so most of the staff were able to catch up on the latest from Wimbledon in the television room, though a number found themselves delighted to take part in an impromptu Scrabble championship organised by Mr Major. Sadly, it all ended in tears when Mr Pickup and Miss Denver nearly came to blows over the former's use of an ill-considered expletive to form a match-winning triple-word score.

For my own part, I took the opportunity to telephone the examination board to complain about the non-arrival of my pay for the SCE marking. After a long and fruitless battle with a clerical assistant at the other end, I demanded to speak to Mr Harvey, the principal examiner for English. I always think that going straight to the top is the best way to get some action.

He didn't seem pleased to hear it was me, and I think I probably annoyed him unnecessarily with my dressing-down of the exam board's administrative procedures which, to be fair, are not really his concern. Nevertheless, I was surprised to hear his note of concern when I threatened to withdraw my labours from marking SCE scripts next year if my payment failed to arrive very soon.

'Oh, don't do that, Mr Simpson,' he oozed down the telephone line. 'I simply can't *imagine* what we'd do without you.'

In retrospect, I might have been more sensitive to what was

obviously well-concealed sarcasm, but at the time I took him at face value.

'Well, that's all very well, Mr Harvey,' I crowed, sensing an advantage, 'but you might *have* to do without me. I can't afford to give up my time marking scripts if these people –'

'And I can't afford,' he snarled in interruption, 'to give up *my* time listening to half-baked complaints about late payments from one of the most incompetent markers it's been my displeasure to come across since I started doing this job!'

'But –'

'– and before you go any further, let me tell you that you'll get your money – eventually – though goodness knows why, seeing as I had to personally re-mark over half your scripts myself. I couldn't help wondering if you'd even *read* most of them in the first place! And as for withdrawing your labours, I should think it highly unlikely that you'll have the *chance* to offer your services for SCE marking next session – at least, not if I've got anything to do with it.'

I tried to stutter a response, but was interrupted by his valedictory enquiry.

'And one final thing, Mr Simpson – what was that appalling stench that kept coming off your exam papers?'

I started to outline the unfortunate incident with the scripts, my school cleaner, and the fish-heads in the kitchen dustbins last month, but got no further than the first explanatory words.

'On second thoughts,' Harvey concluded, 'I don't really think I want to know. Good-bye, Mr Simpson. Your cheque's in the post, as they say . . .'

I put the telephone down. What a rude man.

Friday

Last day of term. Only seventeen pupils turned up, all of them for free lunches, and all of whom disappeared from sight upon the bell ringing to start afternoon lessons.

It was all a rather anti-climactic end to the session, really, and I couldn't help but make comparison between Mr Pickup and myself as we prepared for our respective summer holidays.

There was I, just managing to fit in an afternoon session with my industrial placement tutor, who was in school to give me details of the hotel I would be attending for management training. This, I confess, came as something of a disappointment: I had expected to be placed – as the brochure had hinted would be the case – in a major city-centre venue, at the heart of international commerce and decision-making. Alas, my fortnight is to be spent in a fairly minor two-star hotel in an east-coast holiday resort – hardly what I would call a thrilling introduction to the world of big business and industry. Still, I suppose even Lord Forté had to start somewhere.

Mr Pickup, on the other hand, spent most of the afternoon leafing through his copy of a tome entitled *The Rough Guide to Italy*, which book he fondly imagines to be sufficient preparation for his two weeks in the sun with a group of fifth and sixth-year pupils. This sordid text apparently reveals the venues where he and his charges are most likely to be able to 'whoop-it-up', as he explained during our farewells at four o'clock.

'Yep, Simpson – I can't wait,' he elaborated. 'Fourteen days on the beach, and fourteen nights in the disco. Some fun, heh?'

I shuddered. 'But where's the educational value?' I asked him pointedly.

'Are you kidding?' he nudged me suggestively in the ribs. 'Have you *seen* some of our sixth-year girls recently? I'm hoping to broaden my education a great deal, old son!' he leered as he made his way to the car park.

'Have a nice time, then,' I called after him as I headed for the bus stop.

'You too, Morris. Have fun in your hotel,' he laughed across the playground. 'I think you'll make a lovely chambermaid!'

I raised my eyes heavenward. Pickup just doesn't seem to realise the value of this industrial placement for my future career prospects – I think he could be laughing on the other side of his face come the new session.

July

AREN'T YOU SUPPOSED TO BE A GIRL?

As he has already indicated, Morris Simpson's application for an industrial placement demonstrated a willingness – touching to the outside observer – to do *anything* to gain promotion.

It has often been a charge levelled at teachers that they set great store on preparing their adolescent charges for 'the outside world', without actually having been in it themselves. It is sometimes felt that too many of them have spent their lives in a an experiential chain of school/university/and back to school again, a life-pattern which can lead to a certain ignorance of any other form of being.

Industrial placements, it was felt, could help to rectify the position, giving many teachers a new perspective on their own jobs and the way they prepared pupils for this outside world. A lot of teachers applied for such placements, usually during the school term. Some, like Morris Simpson, chose to give up their holiday time as well. Towards the end of July, after a three-week opportunity to recharge his mental batteries, Morris reported for duty.

Monday

This has been the first day of my fortnight's industrial placement, and even now I am beginning to regret the entire venture. It had already been a major source of disappointment to learn that my management experience in the leisure industry was to be based in a rather downmarket seaside hotel on the east coast, but I was completely unprepared for the seedy welcome I received from the even seedier proprietor of the Imperial Grand Hotel – a misnomer if ever there was one.

Having approached a cramped reception desk in the corner of what laughingly passed for an entrance hall, I coughed to gain the attention of a rather scruffy-looking individual who was slouched over a copy of yesterday's *Sunday Sport*, a cigarette dangling from the corner of his mouth. He looked up.

'Yeh? Can I help?'

Drawing myself up to my full height, I gave an appropriately dismissive look: 'I've an appointment with Mr Hastie, your general manager. I'm here on an –'

'That's me,' he interrupted.

'Yes, well I'm here on –' I continued, before realising what he had said. '*You're* Mr Hastie?' I asked in disbelief. 'Mr Hastie, the manager?'

'Very same,' he confirmed. 'And who are you?'

'Um . . . Simpson,' I explained, rapidly pondering the wisdom of my placement liaison officer in sending me here, 'Morris Simpson, Parkland High School – I'm here for a fortnight.' I offered a handshake, but Mr Hastie had buried his head in a host of assorted letters and paperwork.

'Simpson, Simpson,' he was muttering to himself, '– don't recall anyone of that name booking in. Is it bed and breakfast only, mate, or were you planning on full board?'

'No, no,' I corrected him. 'I'm not here as a guest. I'm here for an industrial placement.'

'Ah!' he smiled in recognition. 'The work experience?'

'Well, not really,' I corrected him again, but he had frowned an interruption.

'Hang on a minute,' he queried. 'Aren't you supposed to be a girl?'

Momentarily nonplussed, I opened my mouth but was unable to frame a suitable response. Mr Hastie went on to explain that of course he was expecting someone from Parkland High School, but that *his* understanding of the arrangement was that a fourth year girl was coming on work experience rather than a member of staff on industrial placement. Yes, he agreed, he was more than happy to have *anyone* around who could help out with making up beds and suchlike, but he wasn't sure if that was what I was really after.

'It certainly isn't!' I scolded him. 'I'm giving up a fortnight of my holidays, Mr Hastie, and it's with the intention of gaining mangerial experience in the leisure industry. If you think –'

'All right, all right,' he held up his hands in surrender. 'I'll see what I can do.'

I think I was quite correct to get angry. You sometimes need to deal sternly with these people.

Anyway, the upshot of it all was that Mr Hastie suggested I unpack my suitcase, after which he would put me in charge of the reception desk for the rest of the afternoon and evening. Having eventually located the glorified broomcupboard which is apparently to serve as my bedroom, I did as requested and reported for duty – looking, I might add, a good deal smarter than the proprietor in my dark waistcoat and matching tie. Actually, it was quite enjoyable, if a little tiring (Mr Hastie had to go out for the evening and didn't relieve me until well after midnight). Still, at least I'm in a quasi-managerial position, and Mr Hastie has promised to go over the financial intricacies of hotel management with me tomorrow.

Tuesday

Portering duties! Mr Hastie was called away on urgent business this morning and claimed that his usual porter had failed to turn up. Would I mind, he asked 'just filling in – until tomorrow, at any rate . . .'

It was difficult to refuse the man in his hour of need, and he did provide a proper porter's coat, so I relented, on the strict under-standing that tomorrow would allow me the chance to investigate the hotel industry from a more elevated position. He agreed, but then rushed away so quickly that I forgot to ask him for a change of bedroom – I was roused from my slumbers at half past five this morning by the noise of kitchen refuse being emptied beneath my window, after which the duty chef's repeated and futile attempts at a vocal rendition of the chorus from *Nessun Dorma* ensured, quite literally, that a return to sleep was impractical.

Wednesday

Today saw the arrival of my long awaited cheque from the examin-ation board, sent on to the Imperial Grand by my mother. At first, I thought the amount payable must have been a down-payment, but a telephone call to the board's administration assistant assured me that the cheque represented the total sum due for the hours of labour which I had endured in marking over three hundred examination scripts for the Higher grade literature exam.

'But that's an appalling rate!' I told the woman on the other end of the line. 'It works out at less than a pound per hour.'

'Well, I gather, Mr Simpson,' she replied, 'that some people manage to get throught their scripts a little more quickly than others. And it's the same rate for everyone.'

That settles it. I shall certainly refuse to be involved with SCE marking *next* year.

More bitterness with Mr Hastie. He has refused to reallocate me a different room on the absurd pretext that a sudden rush of guests might fill up the twelve other empty rooms – he should be so lucky. And my dignity suffered an even greater blow today when he absolutely insisted that I 'help out the girls' by serving in the dining-room. I eventually agreed, and was absolutely mortified to have an old-age pensioner press a ten pence piece into my palm after being served with afternoon tea.

'There you are, sonny,' she simpered across the remnants of her buttered scone. 'You'll make a *lovely* waiter . . .'

Thursday

A national scandal has erupted over Mr Pickup's Italian holiday with the fifth and sixth year! I first became aware of it as I was serving a family with breakfast this morning (the dining room is still short of a waitress). Leaning over Mr Barton's table to retrieve a toast rack and replace his pot of tea, my eye caught a glimpse of the headline in his copy of the *Daily Mail*.

'Good grief!' I spluttered, unfortunately catching the teapot handle as I drew myself up in surprise. Mr Barton let out an oath of displeasure as a potful of scalding tea cascaded down his trousers, but I was too concerned with grabbing his newspaper to do anything other than mutter a brief apology.

'SCHOOL MASTER'S DRUNKEN BRAWL WITH FIFTH YEAR LOVELIES!'

proclaimed the front page of the journal, before going on to explain that a 'so-called educational holiday' from Parkland Community High School had turned into a 'constant round of drunken midnight revelries', apparently organised by staff for the enjoyment of the pupils. Chief culprit, according to the reporter, was geography and religious education specialist David Pickup – or rather 'David Drink-up', as the story subsequently labelled him. He, it appeared, was the man behind the late-night party which had yesterday culminated in the group's permanent exclusion from three local disco-theques as well as a bill for several million lira from the hotel at which Pickup is based – the result, apparently, of an over-inebriated sixth year pupil launching himself full force into a plate-glass window.

Even allowing for the excesses of tabloid journalism, it looks a serious business, and I can't help but observe that I'd already warned Pickup of the likely dangers attending this trip. Sadly, the man has little sense of responsibility towards his pupils, a fact which was confirmed by the newspaper's front-page picture of my bronzed professorial colleague, his arms draped around two of the senior girls at the same time as he toasted the anonymous photographer with a king-size grin and a can of continental lager. 'Cheers, Sir!' read the caption: 'Party Time for David Drink-up – the oldest swinger in town . . .'

I cringed inwardly, then woke from my reverie as Mr Barton made a further impatient demand for a cloth to wipe his trousers. I scurried back with it, just in time to witness him jabbing a finger at his newspaper's front page and making a string of bitterly directed remarks about teachers. He seemed to be suggesting that most members of the profession were so inept that it would be beyond their logistical talents to organise a large-scale party in a brewery. Actually, given the nature of Pickup's latest indiscretion, I thought his contention to be inaccurate, on this occasion at least, but kept my reflections to myself. Similarly, I refrained from explaining my own educational position – not to mention my own friendship with Pickup. In the hotel business, it sometimes pays to be discrete.

Friday

An awful day. It began with an altercation between myself and Mr Hastie. Not only have I yet to receive any real instruction in the art of leisure management, but this morning he plumbed new depths by asking me to perform a series of operations more normally undertaken by a chambermaid; indeed, when he ordered me to make up sixteen beds and ensure that 'all the bedroom toilet-pans are sparkly-bright and fit to eat your dinner off,' I was on the point of handing in my resignation!

The day worsened considerably after morning coffee with a disastrous set of new arrivals to the hotel, in the shape of Mr and Mrs Carswell, along with daughter Janie! The chairman of the school board was the last person I wanted to meet in this lowly position, and I could well have done without his discovery that my placement has turned out to be a disastrous example of the industrial links which we educationists are so keen to forge.

Alas, secrecy proved impossible, as I was asked to serve at table during the lunchtime immediately subsequent to their arrival.

The look of surprise on Carswell's face was soon replaced by an expression of infinite and malicious mirth, and it was all I could to to remain civil in the face of repeated and peremptory requests for the tomato ketchup and brown sauce with which he appears wont to smother every article of carefully prepared food that is set before him.

'Well, well, Mr Simpson,' he eventually belched at the end of his second helping of rice pudding. 'Didn't expect to find *you* having to take a summer job for some extra cash. Is this *allowable* under your conditions of service? I mean, aren't you *getting* paid for these six weeks of holiday already?'

I reminded him brusquely of our conversation at last month's prizegiving, and that my appearance at the Imperial Grand was an integral and essential part of the industrial placement scheme with which I hoped to enrich my curricular awareness at Parkland High School. His snorted rejoinder of disbelief was too much to bear, and I am afraid that I rather opened myself to his further displeasure by observing my own surprise at finding him resident for his summer holidays in such a disreputable flea-pit, where hot and cold running water seemed to be an optional extra in most rooms.

Needless to say, immediately after lunch he reported my indiscretion to Mr Hastie, who lost no time in announcing the early conclusion of my placement – just a moment, alas, before I was able to have the pleasure of offering my resignation myself, on the grounds of worker exploitation.

'You bloody teachers!' he swore at me. 'You're all the same – see a bit of hard work, and you'll run for miles to avoid it!'

I was about to contradict him severely when I heard Mr Barton's exclamation of disbelief from the corner of the dining-room, where he and the Carswell family were deep in earnest conversation: 'You're kidding!' shouted Barton in response to Mr Carswell's most recent revelation, and pointing in my direction. '*That's* a teacher? Come off it! You *must* be joking . . .'

I threw my fiercest look in their direction, swung on my heel and strode upstairs to pack my suitcase. Perhaps I should have joined Pickup after all – at least I might have got a sun-tan!

August

The industrial placement was not, it has to be admitted, a significant success. Fortunately for Morris at the start of the new session, news of his disastrously abortive secondment was overshadowed by the emerging details of what had *really* gone on during Mr Pickup's Italian trip.

Back at Parkland, the new term began for Morris in much the same dispirited fashion as the last one had ended and – despite his inherently optimistic outlook – he once again found himself occasionally questioning the validity of his vocational yearnings. Teaching could sometimes be a real pain in the backside.

At least there was the prospect of some new staffroom furniture to brighten the outlook from within: some new chairs, a microwave oven and – a year after his initial promise – Mr Ross had at last managed to secure a new staffroom pool table.

And there was also, Morris kept reminding himself, the return of Fiona Strangelove to anticipate with relish. Not to mention, so he understood, the imminent arrival of a new assistant headteacher: rumour had it that this man was a more innovative educationist than Bob Major (not that that was saying much), and Morris hoped that here he might find an ear more sympathetic to his own educational ambitions.

But this is to anticipate. Morris's diary for August takes up the story some time after the summer holidays had ended.

Monday

Two weeks into the new term, and already the summer holidays seem light years away.

The stink about Mr Pickup's disastrously disciplined trip to Italy with the fifth and sixth years seems to have died down, although the headmaster is still having to deal with a string of parental complaints which, he assures us, will mean that Pickup is never, ever, let loose on such a quasi-educational excursion again. The last straw seems to have been a fifteen-a-side mixed football match which a senior boy organised in the couchette accommodation of the overnight channel ferry which returned the party to our shores.

Understandably, other passengers were seriously inconvenienced by the fixture and one or two appeared incontinent with rage to discover that Mr Pickup, as party leader, seemed unable to drag himself away from the ship's cocktail bar until well after closing time, by which hour the game in question had concluded in a twelve-all draw. Mr Pickup tells me he intends to maintain a much lower profile this session. We shall see.

Otherwise, life at Parkland Community High School remains much as before. Mr Ferguson is still refusing to have anything to do with the primary school liaison project in modern languages on the grounds that he has never been trained for 'wet-nursing a bunch of over-excitable wee girls – and that's just the teachers in the place!' He is swift to condemn.

We have at last fallen heir to a brand new staffroom pool table, not to mention a gleaming microwave oven to augment the somewhat primitive cooking conditions which had hitherto pertained. Actually, it's proving impossible for everyone to get a fair chance at using either: there are massive queues for re-heating a voluminous assortment of ready-made meals at lunch-time (a nutritionally suspect means of food preparation, in my opinion, though Miss Tarbet from home economics always seems first in line); and with regard to the pool table, you might know that Frank Parker (physics and acting APT guidance), along with a bunch of his cronies from PE and technical, spend practically every waking hour on the damned thing. It's quite ridiculous: they have a rota to ensure that one of them abandons a class two minutes before lunch every day and sneaks into the staffrom to secure the table with a string of twenty-pence pieces which will see them through the next sixty minutes at least. Meanwhile, the rest of us have to endure their pathetic whoops and squeals of triumph and anguish as they imagine themselves in the top flight finals of a professional snooker tournament – and àll on a six foot long pastry-board!

When do they prepare their lessons? That's what I want to know!

Tuesday

A staff meeting after school, wherein the headmaster took the opportunity to renew his annual request that the staffroom tea-urn be switched off between intervals. I really don't know why he bothers any more: although he seemed deadly serious about it, I expect his warnings to meet with the same response as they have in the six years since I started teaching here. To whit: none at all.

Otherwise, the meeting was notable for Mr Ross's formal introduction of two new members of staff who had joined us in the second week of term.

Firstly, he indicated the presence in the front row of our new assistant head teacher, Richard Dick.

'Good God!' spluttered Pickup rather too loudly for comfort: 'I don't believe it! Dick Dick!' So much for his low profile, I thought, as several eyes (including Mr Dick's) turned in the direction of the back row where Pickup and I had ensconced ourselves.

I was somewhat concerned to realise that not a few members of staff were obviously unable to discern whether the source of the outburst had been Pickup or myself. My blushed realisation of their uncertainty no doubt led Mr Dick to have his doubts as well, especially given Pickup's innocent look of enquiry in my direction, looking for all the world as if he hadn't quite caught whatever I'd just said. I was furious, and blushed even more, which probably made matters worse. So much for friendship.

Mr Ross, however, is a past master at the art of getting through awkward moments at staff meetings, so he immediately moved on to his second introduction: 'this time of Fiona Strangelove, a figure –' and here I thought he stressed the word 'figure' rather too strongly '– who is already well known to us from her student days at Parkland.'

He then asked Fiona – as devastatingly attractive as ever – to stand up so that we could all see who she was, a means of identification which he had thought unnecessary to suggest for Mr Dick. The poor girl was understandably embarrassed to have 54 pairs of eyes burning into her – and I confess that few burned more fiercely than my own. Recollections of abortive attempts to ask her out last term fled from my mind, as an anciently-recalled passion stirred in my loins.

'Get your filthy eyes off her, Simpson,' whispered Mr Pickup in my ear. 'I told you last session – she's out of your class.'

I uncrossed my legs and told him that I didn't know what he was talking about.

Wednesday

Great news. I'm to team-teach class 2F with Fiona Strangelove. Simon Young announced the arrangement at our departmental meeting this morning, and asked us to 'get together as soon as possible to work out who does what.' Fiona didn't look too enthusiastic at the prospect, but I found it difficult to control my heartbeat.

However, as I told myself at lunchtime, I mustn't appear too eager. The staffroom, in fact, is becoming uncomfortably hot and crowded during lunch hour: the condensation on the walls from the continually boiling tea-urn doesn't help, of course, and the queues at the microwave grow ever longer. I have contented myself by making renewed arrangements for bringing in a pack of cheese sandwiches which at least means I can finish eating before the end of the break. Today, of course, they tasted so much the better as I gave private and contemplative thought to the prospect of sharing a few dramatic improvisations with class 2F – and Fiona Strangelove, of course.

Thursday

Mr Ross's concern over the ever-simmering tea-urn has obviously reached ungovernable proportions, because he has at last taken draconian action.

His disciplinary redress has taken the form of removing the black ball from our new staffroom pool table, thereby rendering all games incapable of conclusion. A large notice was appended to the table bearing an ultimatum which brooked little negotiation:

WHEN THE TEA-URN GOES OFF
THE BLACK BALL COMES BACK!
Signed: J Ross.

It was a stroke of genius. Parker and company came bouncing in as usual at lunchtime like a pack of overgrown schoolboys, only to discover their precious pool tournament to be strangled at birth. The oaths and deprecations which followed were most unbecoming to a mixed staffroom but the eventual outcome, unsurprisingly, was the immediate unplugging of the tea-urn and a loudly-mouthed injunction from Parker that it be *left* switched off between intervals – 'or there'll be blood on the walls, I can tell you!' he concluded threateningly. What can you expect from a physics teacher?

Whereupon he scuried off to Mr Ross's study to ask for his ball back. Sadly, Mr Ross was away to a Rotary lunch and had left word that he would be unlikely to return before 3pm. He's cleverer than I thought.

Friday

Mr Dick looks like making his presence felt. He has launched himself into his new AHT role with what appears to be accustomed gusto and seems intent upon shaking everyone up, whether they like it or not.

'God save us,' muttered Pickup at morning break, as we overheard Mr Dick speaking to Mr Ferguson, head of modern languages. 'We've got a whizz-kid here, y'know.'

Tuning in to the conversation across the coffee table, I began to see what he meant. Mr Dick has been assigned the position of assistant head in charge of curriculum development and primary liaison, which explained his immediate attempts to ingratiate himself with Mr Ferguson. I think he may soon consider himself to have been handed a poisoned chalice, if Mr Fergson's initial remarks were anything to go by.

'Listen, sonny,' laboured Jack Ferguson (hardly a very respectful form of address, even if Mr Dick *does* look positively pubescent): 'I've been teaching for 26 years now; I *wanted* to retire two years ago and they wouldn't let me. And it was all this 'languages in the core' nonsense that kept me back. Now they're trying to get them into the primaries as well. Forget it, son. I was down at our feeder primary only last term, and I don't want to repeat -

'Associated primary, actually, Mr Ferguson,' corrected Mr Dick. 'We call them associated primaries now, not feeder primaries.'

'Oh, do we now?' Jack Ferguson raised his eyebrows. 'And why would that be, pray tell?'

'Well,' enthused our new assistant head, clearly unable to detect a sarcastic enquiry at 15 paces, 'an *associated* primary school implies that we're working in *association* with that school – you know, working towards the same goals and all that; the term 'feeder' primary, on the other hand, smacks of a hierarchy and belittles the effort of the primary school: it suggests that pupils going into secondary are being 'fed' into a school which is in some ways better, and that they're going 'further up' in the hierarchy of education.' His point made, he smiled along the coffee mugs.

Ferguson looked blank. 'And aren't they?' he queried. 'I thought that was the point of secondary education?'

I think Mr Dick might have his work cut out.

Unfortunately (as it all turned out) I finally got a chance to use the microwave oven today. This being Friday, the staffroom was practically deserted at lunchtime, most of my colleagues having departed to The Pig and Whistle for their regular session of curriculum development. Consequently, I had saved a portion of last night's lasagne in a frozen food container and was able to pop it in for a spot of quick reactivation at Power Level 10 just as the lunch hour started. Unfortunately, I nipped back to my classroom after setting it in motion to retrieve a set of third-year jotters for some lunchtime marking, and was further delayed in my return by attempts to call a halt to a serious outbreak of water-bombing by some over-exuberant first-years.

It was to my horror, therefore, that I returned to the staffroom to witness a display of fearsome pyrotechnics from my rapidly overheating lasagne, which was still circulating at a rate of knots on the oven's turntable. Sharp tongues of lightning appeared to be licking all around the edges of my erstwhile meal, and the whole caboodle looked set to erupt in flames at any minute.

It was much later before I discovered that I had programmed the wretched machine for a 30 minute session instead of a quick three-minute burst. And it was later still when I discovered that, of all things to use in a microwave oven, foil containers are possibly the worst, causing, as they do, a whole host of electromagnetic special effects. Fiona Strangelove, who had gallantly come to my rescue in pulling the microwave's plug from the wall and had sub-sequently calmed my panic, then proceeded to give me a stern lesson in the cooking techniques of modern cuisine. Unfairly, it culminated in her rather ill-judged assertion to the other returning staff that, as 'Mr Simpson was the bloody oaf responsible for busting up the microwave, then Mr Simpson should bloody well replace it out of his own pocket.'

I protested my innocence, as well as my inability to pay, but some of the staff looked pretty ferocious.

I'm sticking to cheese sandwiches in future.

September

WEEF

The financial implications of purchasing a new staffroom microwave were really beyond the salary boundaries of an unpromoted member of staff such as Morris Simpson. Fortunately, the regional insurance policy promised to pay up, but Morris experienced a worrying few weeks of insecurity beforehand.

He was also, of course, continually subject to bouts of severe depression concerning his working conditions – so much so, in fact, that he had actually considered applying for a 'job-share' to ease his stress-level. Actually, this regional initiative was more properly designed with female teachers – especially mothers – in mind and was intended to to alleviate the problems of shrinking teacher-supply in a workforce where there was an entirely different sexual balance to that which had existed some 30 years previous. Job-sharing would give such women the chance to remain as fully-fledged employees of the education authority, albeit working on a part-time basis, while still allowing them the chance to devote time to their infant families – or whatever other interests they wished to pursue. For teachers like Sandra Denver – just starting her second successive bout of maternity leave in two years – the eventual chance to job-share would be a real boon; for just now, she looked forward to another happy issue the following spring.

The 'up-side' of job-sharing was the fact that teachers would only have to see their pupils for half of the working week; the 'down-side', of course, was the fact that they would consequently receive only half of their salary cheque at the end of the month. For this reason, if for no other, Morris's application to job-share was never likely to be made.

In any case, he reminded homself forcefully, working for only half of the week would cut by exactly 50% the amount of time he was able to spend in the company of Fiona Strangelove. Foolishly, and against all indications to the contrary, he still found himself irredeemably infatuated with the girl.

As his diary entry for September will reveal, Morris was still attempting to impress Fiona with a few carefully prepared worksheets; unfortunately, the normally efficient service which he had come to expect from the school office appeared to have been suspended.

Monday

Dropped off some worksheet notes to the office on my way into school this morning, and was distressed to be greeted by a gum-chewing adolescent female who was standing in the place of our normal clerical virago, Mrs Thomas.

'Aye?' the girl slurred across the paperwork I handed over the counter. 'Whit d'ye want me tae dae with *these*?'

'Well, type them up, of course – um . . . ?' – in vain I waited to have her give me a name, but she seemed rather slow on the uptake.

'Ah, that's Michelle, Mr Simpson,' explained Mrs Taylor, the office second-in-command. 'She's with us for the rest of this week as a temporary replacement –'

'Aye,' confirmed the girl. 'But ah canny type, so ye'll have tae whistle . . .'

'What!' I exclaimed angrily. 'But –'

'I'm sorry, Mr Simpson,' soothed Mrs Taylor, 'but Michelle's more or less correct – though,' she frowned at the new junior, 'she might have phrased her refusal somewhat more politely. Eh, Michelle . . . ?'

'Oh aye,' drawled the unseemly creature. 'S'ppose soa . . .'

Sadly, Mrs Taylor confirmed that the office would be hopelessly short-staffed this week, and that any 'rush-jobs' – as this one was – couldn't possibly be undertaken until next Monday at the earliest. This was a source of some disappointment, as the notes were in preparation for my new batch of team-teaching lessons with the delectable Fiona Strangelove and 2F, and consisted of a host of dramatic improvisation topics surrounding our new project on gangs and violence. It starts on Wednesday, so I'll just have to write them on a Banda sheet instead. It won't look as impressive to Fiona as a typewritten affair – but at least she'll see the benefits of being properly prepared for a junior class.

I was discussing Michelle's apparent lack of office skills with Mr Pickup at lunchtime, and he agreed wholeheartedly with my assessment of the girl.

'Yep – she's absolutely useless,' he confirmed. 'I asked her to photocopy some workcards and even *that* was beyond her, according to Mary Taylor. Told me the girl can hardly read, never mind write, and that the only task she'd successfully completed this morning was to make herself seven cups of coffee between the hours of 9am and 12 noon

'Honestly!' I scoffed in reply. 'It's quite disgraceful, a secretarial supply company sending along someone like that – or even taking her on to their books in the first place! Can't type, can't work a photocopier, can't read and can't even write! Where do they get them from, I wonder?'

'Oh that's simple enough,' Pickup explained quickly. 'She's one of our former pupils.'

'What?'

'Yep – left two years ago with three SCOTVEC Certificates in interpersonal communication and a Parkland High Leaver's Card that told the world she'd successfully completed two and a half learning-skill modules.'

'What *in*, for heaven's sake?'

'Dunno,' Pickup shrugged his shoulders. 'Making coffee, I suppose . . .'

Tuesday

Mr Ferguson's primary languages project continued apace today, but with a much more successful outcome than last term.

Apparently, there have been a number of new staffing appointments at Parkland Primary School, not least the teacher of Primary 6, with which class Mr Ferguson spends much of his liaison time, and it was with a spring in his step that he entered the staffrom during the lunch hour.

'Well?' enquired Mr Dick, our youthful new assistant head-teacher, 'How did it go?'

'Tremendous, thanks,' smiled Jack Ferguson. 'A real triumph, actually. They've got a new teacher there that I'm working with, and she's more in line with my way of thinking.'

'Oh?' we asked in chorus.

'Yes. Doesn't try and stick her nose in to what I'm doing with them for a start, and – more important – doesn't put up with any nonsense from the little tow-rags. First one to open his mouth when I was speaking today got hammered with two punishment exercises – one each from both of us – and that was that. Plain sailing for the rest of the morning. None of your free expression and wandering round the class copying off each other: just down-to-earth, honest-to-goodness *work*. And d'you know what? They actually seemed to *like* it! I can't wait to get back on Thursday!'

Mr Dick looked a little doubtful upon hearing of such old-fashioned approaches to the teaching of languages, but relaxed a little as Ferguson regaled us with a glowing tribute to the enthusiasm of Primary 6 as they embarked upon this morning's work of pre-tending to purchase twenty eight individual railway tickets between Paris and Nice. It had been a practical task which, Mr Ferguson assured us, would be of immense relevance to their later adult lives.

And who am I to doubt it?

School board meeting tonight, but I have made my apologies, plead-ing pressure of work. This gives the double benefit of continuing to avoid Mr Carswell, the board's chairman (whom I have not met since our rather unfortunate encounter during my work experience during the summer holidays), as well as allowing me the chance to complete my Banda worksheet for 2F – and for Fiona, of course.

Wednesday

My Banda worksheet failed to provoke much enthusiasm from Fiona or, indeed, from class 2F. The only exception was Tommy McShane, who spent the entire lesson inhaling the odour of methylated spirit from his sheet and pronounced the lesson 'a brammer, surr'.

Unfortunately, the rest of the class was more impressed by the fourteen-page booklet produced by Fiona on the school's newly acquired 'Apple-Mac' desk-top publishing facility. It is a striking tome which she plans to use as the basis of our three-week theme study on gangs and violence, and which seems to incorporate an all-encompassing range of reading, talking, listening and writing skills. Having sat and watched me flounder through a five-minute presentation of my own worksheet, Fiona then had the effrontery to instruct 2F to 'put those sheets away now – they'll do for homework if we're stuck.'

I was saddened and surprised to witness such unprofessional conduct from one so newly qualified, but managed to hide my annoyance until after the lesson:

'Really, Fiona,' I chided her in the storecupboard. 'We'll have to work more closely in preparation time – and you'll need to give me a little more warning if you're going to produce material like that. I mean,' I lied frantically, '– I'd just knocked that Banda up a few minutes before the lesson, and it's hardly very fair to shove the second year equivalent of *War and Peace* in front of them as an alternative, now is it?'

'That little workbook!' she laughed. 'I zipped that off yesterday afternoon in my free period. Went down well, I thought – didn't you?'

Sadly, she was correct. My own popularity with 2F – never extensive in any case – seems to be in striking decline, and it is a decline which is in inverse proprtion to Fiona's rapidly increasing popularity. I wonder what I can do to impress her?

Thursday

Fiona's theme study continued with relish today, and I find myself increasingly required to take on the role of supporting teacher, rather than having us work as an effective partnership. This is rather annoying, especially given my seniority over her. I must take the matter up with Simon Young, my temporary principal teacher.

One interesting snippet to emerge from Fiona's discussion with 2F this morning was her particular enthusiasm for men with moustaches. The revelation occurred during a 'character build-up' for one of the key roles in the dramatic scenario she has devised to initiate our – or rather, her – project.

'Mmm,' she agreed to Janie Carswell's suggestion that the gangleader be portrayed with appropriately luxurious growth on his upper lip: 'Good idea, Janie – a moustache always helps to add a sinister air, don't you think? Certainly adds a touch of manliness,eh?'

She moved swiftly on to other topics, but I made mental note of her remarks – and may take future action on them.

In the meantime, Mr Ferguson's world has been shattered by the discovery that Mrs Ritchie, his new-found ally in primary teaching methodology, is only likely to be in attendance on every second visit which he makes to Parkland Primary, as she is part of a job-sharing arrangement.

He had experienced, we gathered, a somewhat unnerving morning at our feeder primary, even believing, at one point, that he had turned up at the wrong school!

'I couldn't make head nor tail of it!' he complained at lunch-time. 'Pamela Ritchie was nowhere to be seen, and neither was the other woman I work with from Primary Seven. Then I had a longer look round the staffroom and realised that there wasn't *anyone* I recognised – except that blooody awful harridan that worked with me last term and who gives the kids free rein to do as they bloody well like!'

We made some sympathetic noises, whereupon he explained his relief at seeing Miss Hatfield, Parkland Primary's headteacher. She, it appeared, had been able to explain to Mr Ferguson that – with the sole exception of herself – the school's entire staff was made up of 'job-sharers', a facility which enables those members of the profession with domestic, or other, responsibilities, the chance to remain in employment while at the same time giving the chance to devote attention to such alternative responsibilities on the days when they are not teaching.

'Or in other words,' barked Jack Ferguson in contempt, 'they're making it easier for part-time housewives to stay in teaching and screw up salary negotiations for true professionals like us! Meanwhile, nobody sees fit to tell me that the entire ruddy staff changes over every Wednesday lunchtime like a set of Navy watchmen and I've got to start all over again with someone who makes Germaine Greer look like a strict disciplinarian!'

Unsurprisingly, his remarks on female teachers, job-sharing or otherwise, started a torrid and vituperative staffroom argument; I kept out of it although, for my own part, I confess to a small measure of sympathy for the man, not least over his confusion this morning. However, I find my credulity more than a little stretched to hear Jack Ferguson described, even by himself, as a true professional in *anything* – especially teaching.

Friday

I've decided to grow a moustache. If memory serves aright, the presence of a moustache has indeed been a common factor in all of Fiona's boyfriends heretofore – or at least, all of the ones that *I've* known about. Left off shaving my upper lip this morning as a start, though it will obviously be a few days before anyone notices any difference.

Meanwhile Mr Ferguson's temper goes from bad to worse, perhaps not without cause on this occasion, which at least had nothing to do with his primary liaison.

To explain, he had experienced great difficulty in forcing entry into his classroom at period four this afternoon. Anticipating some prank from the seniors who use B46 as a common room at lunchtime, he carefully nudged his briefcase around the door to encounter instead a series of large, filled, polythene bags which were blocking the doorway. Further investigation revealed a total of twenty-four such parcels, each containing approximately one stone of frozen chips!

'And they're rapidly defrosting, I can tell you!' he wailed as he called me up from the staffroom to assist in their removal to the school kitchens. There had been, he outlined briefly, a 'major cock-up from the delivery firm, aided and abetted by the school office . . .'

Pressed for further explanation as we both tugged at the neck of one particularly intractable bundle, he grimaced fiercely and swore loudly:

'Bloody Michelle, that's what!'

'Michelle?' I grunted. 'In the office? What's she got to do with it?'

'Only told the delivery man to put them here, didn't she? 'Twenty-four packs of French Fries?' she says to him. 'I think that'll be for the modern languages department – up the stairs, then turn right'. Awfully helpful girl, our Michelle . . .'

I refused to believe him at first. 'Oh, come on, Mr Ferguson: nobody's *that* stupid . . .'

'Don't you believe it, Simpson,' he dragged another package of chips across the floor of his classroom. 'Don't you believe it!'

Poor Mr Ferguson. How all things do conspire against him.

Moustache coming along quite well tonight. My top lip looks quite dark already.

October

Yet another area of Scottish educational provision which became subject to a substantial degree of change (and decay) in the 1990s was that of the advisorate.

The particular arrangements differed from region to region, but a wide-ranging and fundamental restructuring of the advisory service was set in motion at the beginning of the decade which saw many advisers in fear for their jobs – a unique experience for *anyone* working within education, let alone a person so exalted as an adviser. These noble men and women felt themselves to have been in the forefront of curriculum development throughout the previous decade (some more active in reaching the forefront than others, it must be admitted), yet their reward – once the dust of formalising Standard grade arrangements had settled down – was to have it suggested that many of them might now be surplus to requirements.

Of course, it wasn't put quite like that: to begin with, many regions pleaded an absolute inability to finance the in-service courses which the advisers had arranged. Consequently, the courses were postponed, withdrawn, or simply cancelled. Suddenly, people began to ask what the advisers would *do* if they weren't organising courses?

It was but a short and logical step to suggest an overhaul of the entire service. It was an overhaul which would outline new areas of responsibility apart from 'advising': they would become involved with inspecting schools, or rather in 'quality assurance' and 'management accountability', two phrases beloved of the new régimes which were holding directorial sway in Scottish education.

But there would be fewer of them needed. Some took to the offer of early retirement, complete with generous lump sum as encouragement, like ducks to water; others accepted, grudgingly, that they would have to go; and some – like Angela Bowman, Morris's ex-principal teacher – intended to make a fight of it.

The Simpson diaries for October explain the position, as well as outlining the continuing growth of our hero's moustache, not to mention the increasing confusion in class 2F about the precise and differing responsibilities of Fiona and Morris in their 'team-teaching' activities.

Monday

I am becoming increasingly concerned about the team-teaching arrangement which I share with Fiona Strangelove, the attractive new member of the English department. The girl certainly appears to have 2F eating out of her hands, what with the impressively-produced set of workbooks she has devised, not to mention the audio and video productions which the class has started to prepare under her whirlwind direction.

Although I have never been in the back seat, as it were, when it comes to educational innovation, I have found myself increasingly in her shadow with 2F, cast almost in the role of classroom assistant rather than in the position of authority which would befit my many years of teaching experience.

Such were my suspicions, at any rate, and they were confirmed by a conversation which I overheard when passing the 2nd year girls' cloakroom this afternoon:

'What've we goat next, Samantha?' enquired Angela Samson.

'Eh . . . English,' replied her colleague, '– wi' Miss Stranjeluv an' Misturr Simpson.'

'Aw, great!' Angela celebrated, and my heart flared momentarily in pride, before her subsequent comment extinguished it completely: 'It's great that they've brought Miss Stranjeluv in, intit, tae take charge o' Simpy? She's great fun, shure she is?'

I swallowed hard. Simpy! I'd thought that *that* particular nickname had disappeared many moons ago, and it was hard to take its reappearance – not to mention the girls' misunderstanding of the shared responsibility which forms the basis of a proper team-teaching arrangement.

The lesson this afternoon was understandably fraught with tension betwen Fiona and myself, and it wasn't helped by some of the pupils' continuing uncomplimentary remarks about the state of my burgeoning moustache, most of which comments Fiona seemed to find hilariously funny. It's bad enough having cheek from the second year about one's personal appearance, without one of one's colleagues apparently encouraging it!

To take but a single example, Fiona's theme-study on violence has recently taken a historical slant, looking at snippets of aggression as displayed in literary and historical events through the ages. Needless to say, her consideration of Nazi atrocities during the Second World War attracted an unwholesome degree of attention from the likes of Alan McLeary and Tommy McShane, who seemed to delight in drawing a parallel between my own moustachioed upper lip and that of the self-styled leader of the Third Reich. In the dramatic improvisation which concluded Fiona's lesson, they took great delight in goose-stepping across my path, forefingers pressed moustache-like under their noses and waiting for me to react.

I ignored them, of course, but it was hard going with Fiona Wallace egging them on. So much for professionalism!

Tuesday

More disgraceful behaviour from 2F this morning, when I caught two of the boys – McShane and McLeary, as you might imagine – scrawling graffiti across a desk towards the end of the lesson. The literary effort which they had embarked upon consisted of an extremely vulgar piece of rhyme about one 'Adolf Simpson' – a freshly-coined nickname for myself, I believe – and his efforts to grow a proper moustache!

I told them that I would be taking the matter up with Mr Dick (our youthful new assistant head) but it was difficult to catch him at lunchtime, as he was buttonholed by Jack Ferguson, our ageing principal teacher of modern languages who had just returned from his Tuesday visit to Parkland Primary and the primary languages project. Poor Mr Ferguson is still finding it difficult to come to terms with life in the modern junior school: having only last month begun to understand the staffing complexities associated with the job-sharing arrangements so common in the primary sector today, he had spent most of *this* morning trying to squeeze his languages project work in among the plethora of other visiting specialists to the school.

'It was awful,' he jabbed a finger at Richard Dick's chest. 'There was an expressive arts woman arrived at the same time as me for a twenty minute session with the class, swiftly followed by a literacy project bloke who wanted the kids to fill in a questionnaire. After that, Pamela Ritchie tells me that she's sorry, but Tuesday after break is the time when the senior teacher comes in for a spot of personal and social development work, after which the visiting PE teacher has to take them away for half an hour of physical jerks. Then it's their TV programme, followed by a rehearsal for next week's assembly hymns, and finally I should get about ten minutes before lunch with them!'

'Well, I'm sorry, Mr Ferguson –' began Mr Dick, but Jack Ferguson was in full flow by now:

'*You're* sorry?' he said angrily. '*You're* sorry? Not half as sorry as me or Pamela Ritchie. 'With all these visiting specialists and class-room antics to perform,' I asked her, 'when d'you get any work done?' The poor woman just sighed, shrugged her shoulders, and told me they'd managed ten minutes of maths first thing this morning, and with any luck they'd get a bit of language work done in the afternoon.'

'Yes, well –' continued Mr Dick, but again without success.

'Yes, well nothing!' exploded Mr Ferguson. 'Is it any *wonder* these kids can't read or write when they arrive here? As far as I can see, they spend all their ruddy time getting half-baked ideas from a procession of professional helpers, and the other half watching TV programmes and practising assembly readings! As far as today was concerned, my own visit was a complete washout, and I'll need to spend all of my time there on Thursday going over what I'd wanted to do today. It's just not good enough, Dick. Not good enough at all.'

Unsure as to whether Ferguson was addressing him in the familiar or the overly-formal mode, Mr Dick was unable to frame an appropriate reply before Ferguson stormed out of the staffroom muttering something about 'glorified play-schools'.

I decided not to bother Mr Dick with the graffiti on my desks.

Wednesday

A distressing letter from Angela Bowman, my former principal teacher, now Adviser in English for the region.

Sadly, in common with the rest of her advisorate colleagues, she has been forced to cancel all of the forthcoming in-service courses which she had arranged. In particular, I was disappointed to learn that the course for which I myself had signed up ('Alternative Strategies for Teaching Punctuation'), and which was due to start tomorrow, has been completely abandoned. All due, apparently, to a shortage of regional funding.

'Well, really,' I complained to Mr Pickup at morning break, 'it's a bit off when the region's so strapped for cash that they've got to call a halt to all the valuable curricular development that's going on.'

'Well, really,' mimicked Pickup rudely, 'I think it's a bloody good job you won't be wasting more valuable time on another self-justification exercise for Angela ruddy Bowman!'

'Pardon?' I queried him sternly. 'Just what –'

'Oh, come off it, Simpson,' he complained loudly. 'You don't mean to tell me that it's any *loss*, this cancellation of in-service, do you?'

'Well, of course it –'

'Good God, man: waken up your ideas,' he berated me. 'Since when was *any* in-service course anything other than an excuse for: (a) the advisers to show everyone what a jolly good job they were doing in organising in-service courses, and (b) the teachers who actually turned up to the damned things to show the advisers what jolly keen teachers they were in turning up for them? Eh? Tell me that!'

I started a reply, but Mr Pickup continued even more rudely:

'And what's this course you were supposed to be going on, anyway? 'Alternative Strategies for Teaching Punctuation', eh? Hah!' he brayed loudly. 'That's a laugh. I didn't think that the English department *had* any strategies for teaching punctuation, never mind finding alternatives for them – at least if the essays I get handed in to me are anything to go by!'

I began to tell him that the teaching of grammar was a whole-school responsibility, but he was back again, sniping at the Advisorate.

'Listen, Simpson, if you ask me it can only be a good thing that Angela Bowman's courses are being cancelled – and every other such course, come to that. Once they've got no more courses to organise, then maybe all these Advisers will end up being put back in the classrooms where they bloody well belong!'

I thought his views showed a disgraceful lack of respect for the sterling work of the Advisorate, and told him so. To my further regret and disgust, he broke wind extremely loudly, adjusted his trousers, and left the room. He really is the limit.

Thursday

More trouble for Mr Ferguson during his second visit of the week to Parkland Primary School. Apparently, he has fallen even further behind in his primary liaison syllabus, due to the fact that he only had five minutes in which to speak to Primary 6 today.

The alternative attraction on offer this morning was a visiting theatre group who performed an uproarious slapstick comedy for the benefit of the whole school, an affair which they nevertheless upheld as an allegorical treatment of working-class resilience in the face of capitalist oppression. Mr Ferguson had apparently spent a pleasant enough ninety minutes watching it, in company with the rest of the teaching staff – 'a set of highly-paid usherettes,' as he quaintly termed them – but had fallen prey to some inward reflection on the nature of his employment terms during this artistic diversion.

The upshot of it all, at lunchtime today, was his announced intention of applying for a job-sharing position as principal teacher of modern languages. Some of us have our doubts about the likelihood of the staffing department being able to find anyone willing to job-share with a 58-year old head of department who longs for nothing so much as an early retirement, but we kept our thoughts to ourselves.

For my own part, I am more concerned with the continuing disrespect of Tommy McShane and Alan McLeary. I have had to endure further sarcasm from the pair about my altered personal appearance, and have told them I shall not put up with it for much longer. Fortunately, I have the support of Richard Dick in this, for he gave me his personal assurance this afternoon that any further misdemeanours by the boys concerned will merit an automatic suspension.

Friday

Another letter from Miss Bowman, asking about my willingness to attend in-service on a voluntary basis, without travelling expenses and, indeed, making some form of monetary contribution for the privilege of attending. Mr Pickup thinks she must be getting desperate, but I plan to give the matter some serious consideration.

Most of my attention today, however, was taken up with torrid disciplinary proceedings against Tommy McShane and Alan Mc-Leary, the end result of which was anti-climactic, to say the least.

And it had all started off so amicably as well: in an attempt to regain a degree of popularity with 2F, I had taken the unwise decision to 'loosen up' slightly in my dealings with them. It had become apparent to me that Fiona's more informal approach seemed to pay dividends, so I thought to follow suit. The first concrete example of this educational glasnost, then, was my decision to enter the classroom after morning break still drinking my interval coffee (unfinished due to a fraught disagreement with Pickup over the wisdom or otherwise of my paying to attend Angela Bowman's in-service course out of my own pocket). The sight of me drinking coffee, I thought, would let 2F know that I *am* human, that I could be their friend as well as their teacher. Sadly, it was not to be.

Alan McLeary annoyed me intensely as soon as I walked in the door, purporting to have noticed something amiss on my top lip (a reference, I immediately spotted, to the luxuriant growth of moustache now present thereon):

'Surr! Surr!' he squeaked. 'Thur's a wee mark under yur nose, surr. Must be a wee bit o' felt pen, surr . . .'

I smiled indulgently at his humorous attempt, and was about to reply with a similarly jocular remark, when McShane joined in the fun and hit, I admit, something of a raw nerve:

'Naw, naw, 'Cleary,' he chimed in. 'That's jist his eyebrow comin' doon fur a wee drink!'

I lost my temper, alas, and marched the pair of them off to Richard Dick. Incredibly, he appeared to have lost all recollection of his promise to supend them and seemed to find the whole affair amusing in the extreme.

I have given the boys a punishment exercise each instead, and have told them that any repetition of their appalling behaviour will lead to really serious trouble. And I mean it.

November

Angela Bowman – as some readers will recall from the earlier diaries of Morris Simpson – was not a woman to be taken lightly. Hell hath no fury like an adviser scorned, and her eventual reaction to the cancellation of her in-service provision was an aggressive counter-attack aimed at the Directorate, as will become apparent in Morris's diary for November.

However, an alternative source of respite from the cares of the classroom was being arranged by David Pickup: well in advance of the festive season itself, he was trying to engender interest among the staff for a Christmas dinner. A group of teachers on an evening out is an event which is distinctive – and memorable – to all who witness it from an outsider's point of view. Perhaps it is something to do with the sudden release from responsibility, the loosening of metaphorical stays which appears to take place when teachers get together in this communal fashion. It can be an awesome – and occasionally embarrassing – sight, and the staff members of Parkland High School were no different to any others in this respect.

108

Unfortunately, as Mr Pickup was to discover, the enthusiasm of teachers to *have* a good night out is not always matched by a willingness to *pay* for it . . .

Monday

An extravagantly decorated notice adorned the staffroom wall when I entered this morning. It had been placed there, I soon gathered, by Mr Pickup, acting in his role as staff social events convenor. **'GRAND CHRISTMAS STAFF DINNER'** it proclaimed in large red festive lettering. **'The Parkland Country House – Please add names to the list below. Hurry! Hurry! Places strictly limited!'**

'There!' smiled Pickup, standing back to admire his artwork. 'That should bring 'em in!'

'I doubt it,' muttered Bob Major, our ageing assistant head, his gaze narrowly focused on the £25 price-tag attached to the bottom of the hoarding. 'Who d'you think's going to come at *that* price, Pickup?' he queried. 'I think the Queen and the Duke of Edinburgh are likely to be otherwise engaged on the night in question . . .'

'Ha! Ha! Very droll, Mr Major, but I think you'll find it's worth every penny at this place. They do a special 'gourmet menu', and the chef's renowned across –'

'I don't care if it's caviar and oysters from the Brothers Roux, old son, but you won't get many people on *this* staff shelling out that kind of dosh for an end-of-term knees-up.'

'Nonsense,' rejoined Mr Pickup. 'If you're going to have a do, then I always say you should make a proper *go* of it. And if –'

'Yes,' interrupted Major in sombre reflection. 'I think you could be said to have lived up to that particular maxim in the course of your career at Parkland High School . . .'

A host of sordid recollections concerning Mr Pickup's alcohol-induced misdemeanours of recent years passed among our collective thoughts, but Pickup wasn't to be dismayed.

'Oh, come off it, Bob,' he cajoled. 'Give yourself a treat. Bring along the wife. Or the girlfriend!' Mr Major arched a strong frown, but not quickly enough. 'Or both!' laughed Pickup, before turning his exhortatory attentions to me.

'And what about you, Morris?' he slapped me on the back. 'You'd fancy a night of epicurean delights, now wouldn't you?'

I muttered something about consulting my bank manager and scurried away to confront 2F instead. I don't want to discourage Pickup, but £25 does seem a bit steep.

Tuesday

No names on Mr Pickup's list as yet, but he was too distracted to notice the empty columns of paper as he entered the staffroom in bewildered mood at morning break.

'Good grief,' he appeared confused, disbelieving, and was rubbing his eyes fiercely. 'Guess what?' he announced to all and sundry. 'I think I've just seen an Adviser in the school!'

The staffroom cynics joined in the fun, needless to say, before I could proffer accurate explanation.

'You what?' exclaimed Frank Parker. 'Surely not? What was he doing – ?'

'*She*, actually,' corrected Pickup. 'Angela Bowman, no less. And what d'you think she was doing?'

'Drinking coffee, I'd imagine!' burst in Bob Major. 'That's all I've ever seen any Advisers doing in here!'

'Actually, gentlemen,' I interrupted in serious tone, 'Miss Bowman's in to discuss the cancellation of her in-service programme with Simon Young, and –'

'That's it!' chortled Major in high amusement, and about as animated as I've seen him for some time now, '– The Adviser In Search of a Lost Course – a striking new piece of drama from Pirandello. True Theatre of the Absurd! D'you hear what she's trying to get us to agree to? Attendance by all divisional English staff at her own private in-service course, not counting towards professional development time, plus the unique opportunity of paying for the privilege of attending – and all because she's petrified they're going to send her back into a classroom where she belongs!'

'Mr Major!' Angrily, I forgot my position for a moment. 'Miss Bowman is simply intent upon forcing the directorate to acknowledge the serious damage to educational provision which will inevitably follow their cost-cutting exercises in halting in-service courses by showing the genuine demand which exists for such courses from grass-roots teachers. And if they really do plan to curtail the advisory service in the same way, then goodness knows where it'll all end! I for one certainly intend to support her, and I've put my name down for her in-service course already!'

'Yes, well that makes two of you in total,' informed Pickup. 'That's why she's in to see Simon Young – trying to drum up some more support, apparently. And talking of drumming up support – 'his eyes turned towards the Christmas lunch list '– I notice the only name on my list so far is that belonging to the Director of Education. Anything to do with you, Mr Major?' he glared fiercely, but Major just whistled down at his shoes. Nice to see the old boy still has a sense of humour.

Wednesday

Mr Pickup has been forced to change the venue for the Christmas Dinner. His carefully lettered notice has been substantially altered to announce a new venue – a local steakhouse – with a more acceptable price-tag of £15 per head.

'My God,' he was muttering this afternoon as he drew a black felt-pen across the previous arrangements. 'Bloody teachers. You try to organise a decent night out, and look what happens. You'd be better off organising a piss-up at the local cemetery!'

'Well, Pickup,' chimed in Jack Ferguson, principal teacher of modern languages. 'You can't say you weren't warned. And y'know,' he pointed at the newly altered pricing arrangement, 'even that kind of sum's going to annoy some people.'

'You what?' exclaimed Pickup. 'But –'

'Well, Mr Pickup, it's all very well for those of you on full salaries, but those of us who are moving into job-sharing arrangements in the pretty near future will soon feel the financial draught, y'know.'

'*Are* you, Mr Ferguson?' I cut in, recalling his announced intention last month of applying for such a position. 'Did you get a job-sharing post as quickly as that, then?'

'Well, it's still to be finalised, of course, but I've told them at staffing that I want to do it, and I've even given them the name of someone who wants to share with me.'

'Oh?' a chorus of interested – if disbelieving – enquiry met this revelation.

'Yes. Peter Wilson up at Rockston High School's been thinking along the same lines as me apparently, and we reckoned it would make an ideal arrangement – and save the staffing department the trouble of looking for someone else into the bargain.'

That explained a lot. Mr Wilson and Mr Ferguson have broadly similar attitudes towards education: both possess a cherished – and as yet unfulfilled – desire to retire from teaching at the earliest possible opportunity. Saving which, presumably this job-sharing arrangement comes as a second best. Mr Ferguson, having expressed his intentions to the staffing department, seems to think that the arrangement is as good as made. I don't think he fully appreciates how they work along there . . .

Thursday

A memo from Miss Bowman this morning to say that her voluntary in-service course has had to be cancelled due to lack of interest. She is a little annoyed about it, but in an effort to maintain the momentum of her newly-styled 'Save Our Advisory Service' campaign, she has asked all English teachers under her charge to write a spontaneous letter of complaint to the Director of Education about the treatment to which she and her colleagues are currently being subjected. Indeed, so spontaneous has this letter to be that she had attached copies of a suitably-worded 'suggested text' to the memo which urged this epistolary action!

She certainly seems to be well organised, but I think the Director of Education will know it's all a put-up job. He's not *that* stupid.

For my own part, I have decided to splash out £15 in order to attend Mr Pickup's Christmas Dinner. Actually, after my team-teaching period with Fiona this afternoon, I had been going to suggest that she might like to accompany me as my official 'partner' for the evening; however, 2F's appalling behaviour was hardly conducive to any such romantic proposal.

I am still having to put up with their ridiculous and pre-pubescent humour with regard to my struggling new moustache: to take but one example, the boy Tommy McShane – who else? – appeared to have got wind of the proposed staff Christmas dinner and spent most of the lesson loudly advising me to avoid the soup-course at the meal in question, '– just in case yurr musstash gets drooned, surr!'

Unbelievably, Fiona still seems to find such remarks hilarious in the extreme. I decided against my offer for the Christmas dinner. She can pay for herself instead!

Friday

Mr Ferguson's hopes of an early start to his job-sharing arrangements have proved illusory, as I feared they would. I came upon his tightly-clenched figure oozing venom down the telephone line during a free period this afternoon. It soon became apparent that he was speaking to a lady from the staffing department:

'Yes, dear,' he gritted his teeth. 'That's right: I spoke to Mrs Clements yesterday, and she thought it would be perfectly in order, as long as Mr Wilson and I submitted the relevant paperwork before Christmas.'

Ferguson's features hardened as he listened to her reply.

'Well what d'you *mean*, we can't just choose someone to job-share with? Every damned primary teacher I know seems to do it if they can.'

He paused again, as the lady at the other end began to explain – as it later transpired – that job-sharing arrangements for promoted posts such as Mr Ferguson's have to be widely and properly advertised in the region's 'job-sheet' and the national press before an appointment can be made.

'And how long's *that* going to take?' snarled Ferguson. 'I wanted this all sorted out by Christmas, you know.'

His face took on a deepening hue, as he heard of his potential waiting-time:

'What!' he bellowed. 'Next *April!?* I could be *dead* by then, woman, for God's sake. What on earth – pardon?' He paused again. 'Listen, I don't give a tuppeny bit if you've been inundated with job-share applications – why don't you lot in staffing get your fingers out and get something moving for once! If you think I'm – Hello . . . ? Hello . . . ?

'Bloody cheek!' he snarled down the line – most unprofessionally, I thought to myself. 'Damned woman's hung up on me! Anyway, that should get them moving – what d'you think, Simpson?'

I muttered something about his having seemed to put her in her place, though privately I expect him to have put back his likely job-share date by at least eight weeks. I have always understood that it pays little dividend to make enemies in the staffing department.

I was about to leave the room when I noticed yet another amendment to the pricing arrangements for Mr Pickup's staff Christmas dinner, and I lost little time in seeking him out in Hut A56 to confirm the new details.

'That's right,' he sighed wearily. 'I'm afraid I've given up, Morris. A large-scale deputation this morning from half the women on the staff moaning that £15 was *far* too much to pay for a four-course meal. And *they* were backed up, I might add, by five of the senior management team, all bellyaching and whining about 'Christmas being a very tight time financially, and couldn't I find somewhere a bit more reasonable?'. I ask you! And *they're* the ones who are on telephone numbers for salaries!'

I expressed sympathy for his position, and enquired how he had possibly managed to locate a venue which served not four, but five evening courses at a cost of £6–25 per head.

'The local Indian restaurant, Morris,' he replied: 'Where else?

113

We're getting a special deal because the owner's son's in fourth year.'

'Hang on a minute,' I quizzed him. 'Isn't that Rashmani's, the place that was done by the health and safety mob last month?'

'The very place, old son. The Salmonella Palace, as I call it. But *they* want to go there, as long as it's eight quid or under for the entire night including wine, and who am I to disagree? Let them be cheapskates if they want – but I'll tell you this, Simpson: they'll not hold David Pickup responsible for the consequences!'

December

As Christmas approached once more, most of the Parkland staff began to anticipate the short festive break with a sense of visible relief. Of course, not *all* educational endeavours were abandoned, and Mr Dick – as a man who so obviously ate, drank and slept education – still had some more ideas up his sleeve, even this close to the holidays.

Morris, as we know, had eventually agreed to attend Mr Pickup's Grand Christmas Dinner despite the fact that he had no real affection for the forced gaiety of such events; his personal preference was for the more reflective and dignified surroundings which would pertain at the school's closing church service on the last Friday of term.

And for Mr Pickup, there was the pleasure of knowing that he had at least managed to gather a quorum for the Dinner, even if there was *still* the occasional complaint about the expense involved.

Monday

Preparations are still being made by Mr Pickup, in his role as staff social events convener, for Thursday night's dinner at Rashmani's, the local Indian restaurant. Unbelevably, he is still having difficulty in persuading our thriftier members of staff to attend because of financial considerations:

'Honestly, Morris,' he cornered me at morning break. 'It's taken me the best part of periods one and two to convince Jack Ferguson that £7–50 for a five-course meal including wine represents pretty good value for money.'

I made sympathetic noises, but Pickup wasn't really listening.

'And it's not as if I don't know what'll happen on Thursday,' he complained bitterly. 'Having spent the last five weeks asking me to find the cheapest available eating-out spot for our main social event of the year, he and the rest of the cheapskates will spend the entire evening complaining about the quality of the food. Wait and see if I'm not right!'

'Nonsense, Mr Pickup,' I tried to reassure him. 'I'm sure the night will be a tremendous success.'

He seemed uncertain, but I'm sure that most of the staff will be too full of Christmas spirit by Thursday to make much complaint, no matter how uncertain the fare.

Tuesday

Richard Dick, our youthful assistant head teacher, seems intent upon making his mark. Today saw the launch of his third curricular initiative since he took up post at Parkland last August. He seems to have lost interest in the first two (Cross-Curricular Vocational Support and Adult Remediation Strategies in English) due to a 'lack of customer take-up', as he quaintly explained during a lunch-time conversation with Mrs Cunningham of computing.

'And that's why,' he looked earnestly across the coffee table at her, 'I've decided to begin a new pastoral care scheme which will involve the computing department. Something that will be of real practical use to us in a whole-school context.'

Pickup and I, listening from the corner, lowered our eyes in discreet amusement as Monica Cunningham made suspicious enquiry of his plans, whereupon Mr Dick launched into an impassioned account of the need to drag Parkland High's guidance system into the 20th century. Briefly put, his scheme necessitates the entry of every pupil's guidance records on to a computer data-base which would allow easy and immediate access for guidance staff provided with the appropriate pass-word. He seemed to have a particularly boyish enthusiasm for the concept of providing pass-words, because he kept repeating the phrase throughout his monologue.

Mrs Cunningham, once she had managed to get a word in edgeways, suggested that this was all very well, but how was she supposed to assist him in the implementation of such a scheme when Mr Baxter, the divisional education officer, had removed most of her computing hardware from the school last May, after an ill-judged complaint from her about the computer room's electrical hazards and the lack of proper security for items contained therein.

'Ah, don't worry about that, Mrs Cunningham,' Mr Dick assured her. 'I've had a word with Dan Baxter about all of this, and he's told me that he's more than willing to finance such an innovative scheme from one of his special budgetary allowances. There's always money to be found,' he lowered his voice conspiratorially, 'if you know where to look for it. And of course,' he continued secretively, 'it *would* be nice to have a fully equipped computing department again, now wouldn't it?'

By this time, Mr Dick had taken Mrs Cunningham by the arm and was guiding her gently out of the staffroom to outline the scheme more fully.

'Marvellous,' Pickup stood back in amazement as they left the room. 'There you have,' he raised a finger aloft and pointed it in the general direction of the empty doorway, 'an almost perfect example of line management – and sheer bloody bribery! Monica Cunningham gets her computers back from Dangerous Dan Baxter, while Dick Dick gets all the credit for launching a technologically innovative guidance scheme – *which*,' he emphasised sharply, 'Monica's going to do all the work for! First art of school management, Morris – delegate the work down the line, but be ready to grab the glory if your plan's a success!'

'And if it's not?'

'Sweep it under the carpet, forget about it. Everyone else will have. Take a lesson, old son,' he wagged an admonitory finger at me, '– that's how you get on these days . . .'

Pickup always sees things in such a cynical light, but he deflected my remonstration to this effect:

'Cynical?' Pickup raised his eyebrows in innocence. 'Not me, Morris. Other way around, in fact: too damned sincere for the likes of Dick, with all his wheeling and dealing and whizz-kiddery! That's why I've never been promoted properly,' he concluded, firm in incontrovertible self-belief. 'Too damned straight by half.'

I thought privately that Pickup's lack of promotional opportunity might owe more to his nascent alcoholism than to any misplaced sincerity, but decided to keep my opinions to myself.

Wednesday

More lobbying of Monica Cunningham by Mr Dick at morning interval. He was obviously successful in his efforts, because by this evening's school board meeting he had given a note to Mr Carswell, chairman of the board, announcing an exciting new guidance and computing development for Parkland High School.

Mr Carswell duly announced, of course, that a newly-entitled programme of pupil guidance and record-keeping – 'Computer Related Assistance in Pastoral Support' – had been devised and would be implemented by Mr Dick. Mr Dick, he reported, had arranged for the education department's regional publicity officer to visit the school to ensure that news of our trail-blazing development is accorded fullest coverage in the local and regional press.

Mr Pickup and I, as staff representatives, couldn't help but express the hope that no newspaper reporter would be sober enough to notice the peculiarly apt acronym by which Mr Dick's new scheme is most likely to be known in future, but I don't think Mr Carswell got the point.

He closed the meeting soon afterwards and, in a forced attempt at festive jollity, expressed the hope that he would see us all at the school's closing carol service on Friday morning. Personally, I shall try to keep out of his way.

Thursday

A disastrous staff dinner, as Pickup had predicted.

In fact, there was something uneasy about the whole evening right from the beginning. Possibly, it had something to do with the seasonal ambience which Mr Rashmani had tried to create in the restaurant: his normally dark and secluded alcoves, surrounded by authentic Indian murals, had been most unfortunately festooned with a collection of fairy lights, miniature reindeer and large plastic models of Father Christmas. In addition, Mr Rashmani seemed intent upon alternating the usual aural accompaniment of Indian sitar music with a somewhat incongruous selection of Phil Spector Christmas songs plus the occasional Johnny Mathis thrown in for good measure. It was all most distasteful, and seemd to offend the sensibilities of Miss Dowling, our head of music, for one.

Her uncomplimentary remarks, however, were as nothing compared to the comprehensive attack mounted by Miss Tarbet (home economics) upon the standard of food presentation and content.

'Ugh,' she winced as she forced her second (and final) fork-full of Mr Rashmani's extra-mild curry across her palate: 'I've tasted better curries from the third-year soc and voc rejects!'

'Same here!' agreed Jack Ferguson. 'There's a hell of a funny taste about it, isn't there, Morag?'

Jokes about horsemeat, not to mention the alsatian which Mr Major had noticed lingering too near the kitchens, soon began to fly thick and fast, much to the embarrassment of the evening's co-ordinator, Mr Pickup. To his credit, he stoically refused to comment, except to throw me knowing glances at every course, glances whose import was confirmed as he took me aside just after the sweet course had been served.

'What did I tell you?' he muttered in my ear. 'It's the same every year: try to organise a decent night out, and they all moan it'll cost too much. So I change the venue to a carry-out joint with seating, and they spend the entire night bleating and whining that it's 'not very good, is it?' Honestly! It'd make you sick! Fancy a job as social convener, Morris?'

I declined his offer and forced down the last of my banana fritter. Actually, I couldn't help but agree with the comments of my colleagues about the quality of food on offer, but I kept my thoughts to myself lest I annoy Mr Pickup. This was probably just as well, for he soon found further cause for agitation as he tried to collect the moneys due to him in payment of the bill.

'Oh, hang on a minute!' squeaked Mrs Cunningham: 'I didn't have the fried rice, you know.'

'Me neither,' affirmed Mr Major. 'It's forty pence less with the boiled rice, Pickup.'

'What?' gasped Pickup. 'What d'you mean?'

'Well, we only had *boiled* rice,' repeated Mr Major, 'and you're asking us for the same as the folk who had *fried* rice . . .'

'Well, of course I am!' rasped Pickup. 'You don't expect me to go round everyone here and total up their ruddy –'

'And I didn't have any wine,' bleated Miss Tarbet. 'I'm not paying for wine that I didn't have, surely?'

'And don't count my pudding in,' complained Miss Dowling. 'Because I didn't have one.'

'Good God almighty!' swore Mr Pickup at the beginning of an outburst which went on for several subsequent minutes, the import of which was that he had no intention of collating individual bills for each person present, and if anyone found themselves unable to come up with the neccesary contribution (arrived at by the simple expedient of dividing cost by participants), then they could (in his own words) 'get into the frigging kitchen and start washing the bloody dishes!'

A few mutinous comments about lack of parity were soon quashed by Pickup's most ferocious glower as he walked round the tables collecting his dues to pay the total bill of £195–80. It was an unwholesome end to a sorry evening.

'Well, at least the service was good,' said Fiona Strangelove as we gathered our coats in the foyer. 'Perhaps we should have left something for that little waiter . . .'

'Oh, that's all right,' mouthed Miss Tarbet, very obviously pleased with herself. 'I dealt with that for all of us.'

'Did you, Morag?' asked Pickup, his faith in our collective generosity momentarily restored. 'Thanks. I was just on my way to see to him.'

'Oh, no bother,' confirmed Miss Tarbet. 'I left a fifty pence piece under my plate, so he should be O.K.'

'For serving twenty-six people?' Pickup clasped a hand to his forehead and shut his eyes. 'Bloody hell, Morag!' After which deprecation, he gritted his teeth, announced that he wouldn't be joining us in the pub after all, and barged his way into the street as quickly as possible.

'What's wrong with *him* then?' asked Miss Tarbet after the swinging door. 'D'you think I left too much . . . ?'

Friday

A distressing conclusion to the term. Almost half of the staff were absent from school this morning due to a particularly severe bout of gastric disorder which seems to have affected those of us who attended last night's culinary excursion. These collective after-effects seem already destined to be recorded in the folk-legend of Parkland High as 'Rashmani's Revenge' . . .

Personally, I spent an extremely unpleasant night in the bathroom, but decided to struggle into school in case I lost my holiday pay. Perhaps I shouldn't have bothered, because along with those of my colleagues who have a similarly pecunious devotion to duty, I seemed to spend most of the morning in an endless queue for the gents' toilet

Even more foolishly, I considered myself sufficiently recovered to accompany my registration class to the carol service in the local church, during which devotions a twenty-minute period of seated immobility left me in severe discomfort. Alas, I could pay little attention to the minister's sermon – theologically sound as it no doubt was – due to the acute stabbing pains in the region of my nether bowel, signalling, I soon began to realise, the onset of every teacher's dread: an imminent attack of monstrous flatulence in the presence of one's pupils.

It was with some pleasure, therefore, that I welcomed the school orchestra's crashing rendition of 'Chestnuts Roasting On An Open Fire'. It was perhaps slightly inappropriate as an aid to divine worship, but at least the all-encompassing noise served the ideal purpose of concealing the powerful emissions of ululant extravagance which, by now, I felt enforced to set free.

Quietly and sensitively adjusting my seating position at the end of this musical interlude, I was silently congratulating myself on not having 'blown my cover', as it were, when I noticed that half of my registration class – Tommy McShane and Alan McLeary in particular – were holding their noses in distaste. McShane made a grossly irreverent comment which I refuse to repeat in print, while Mr Pickup, in the pew behind, displayed a severe lack of professional etiquette by leaning forward and muttering an oath of displeasure in my left ear:

'My God, Simpson: was that *you*? How long's *that* one been brewing?'

I flushed, but ignored the enquiry. Alas, the minister chose this moment to announce the next item in proceedings:

'The senior choir,' he intoned gravely, 'will now sing the anthem: *Whence Is That Goodly Fragrance?* . . .'

It was all too much for Pickup, not to mention class 2F. An explosion of braying laughter from all concerned ensured the disruption of the entire service and, alas, the enforced wrath of the depute head at a slightly torrid meeting outside the church doors at the end of the service. Understandably, I was unable to discuss the disturbance at any great length with Mr Tod, having urgent needs to consider elsewhere, but he indicated a desire to see me as early as possible in the new term:

'Perhaps, Mr Simpson' he hissed fiercely in my ear, 'we could make an appointment next year to discuss the disgraceful lack of control you seem able to exert over your registration class. Not to mention,' he barked, in cruel afterthought, 'your bowels!'

If this is all the support I can expect from senior management, I don't know why I bother. Talk about peace and goodwill . . .

January

Another Christmas, and another time for reflection by Morris Simpson: sometimes he wondered if Pickup was *right* to try and persuade him to leave the profession. He constantly seemed to end up on the wrong side of the senior management team, and some of the things which went on in education these days left him more than a little bewildered. Try as he might, for example, Morris reckoned he could never emulate someone as dynamic as Richard Dick, who seemed to produce curricular innovations and educational initiatives at the drop of a hat.

And then there were the parent/teacher evenings which were coming up at the end of January. Here was an area in which Morris still felt particularly let down by the lecturers in his teacher-training course all those years ago: he had never really been given any *training* for parents' nights, and he could recall several embarrassing occasions which had arisen as a result of this. In particular, he had never discovered any really practical methods of dealing with the type of garrulous and loquacious parents who would frequently over-run their interview time (at least, that was how Morris viewed the situation), thereby causing immense disruption for other teachers with whom they had successive appointments.

For the parents' evening in January, however, there was a set of parents – Mr & Mrs O'Brien – with whom he wanted to have as full and frank a discussion as time would allow. Their daughter, Rothesay, had arrived in Parkland High as an 'exceptional transfer' from a neighbouring school. She was a difficult child . . .

Monday

Today saw the unhappy arrival of a new pupil in class 2F, the unusually-named Rothesay O'Brien. She is almost certainly the most badly-behaved child I have ever come across, and seems intent upon causing maximum disruption during each and every lesson. Not content with shouting out unbelievably insolent remarks at every opportunity, she frequently bangs her head up and down on her desk, and insists upon falling off her chair if the lesson becomes over-tedious for her twenty-second attention span, after which cacophonous interruption she has a self-abusive tendency to bite her own arm until it bleeds!

In a sense, I feel sorry for the girl, who obviously has severe psychological problems. Parkland High is her third school since last August, and such peripatetic wanderings must be unsettling; nevertheless, her behaviour has had a profound effect on 2F, hitherto a relatively stable unit: I just hope the young madam's parents turn up on Thursday at our parents' evening, so that I can make myself clear about their appalling daughter's unconscionable behaviour.

Meanwhile, Mr Dick's innovative technological guidance scheme – 'Computer Related Assistance in Pastoral Support' – seems to be well and truly off the ground, what with the delivery of a spanking new set of hardware for Monica Cunningham's computing department.

'You see, Mr Pickup,' I chided my colleague from religious education and geography as we walked past Mrs Cunningham's room on our respective ways to Huts A56 and 57. 'Mr Dick's been as good as his word.'

We both peered through the door window and observed Mr Dick gleefully unpacking a dozen gleaming monitor units with keyboards and printers to match. Our youthful assistant head reminded me ever so slightly of a small boy in a sweetie shop. 'If I remember rightly,' I cruelly reminded Pickup of his prophecy last month, 'you reckoned this new scheme would be a nine-day wonder, with Dick chucking in the towel and loading it all on to Monica as soon as the local press had done their feature on him?'

'Pah!' came his scathing rejoinder. 'Wait and see, Simpson. Wait and see . . .'

I don't think Mr Pickup can see the good in *anybody*.

Tuesday

Loud lamentations from Monica Cunningham at morning break, concerning Mr Dick's abandoned involvement with the CRAPS scheme.

'Honestly!' she gritted her teeth in the coffee queue: 'The man's impossible! First of all, he wheedles me into a fully-fledged commitment to helping *him* organise a computer assisted guidance scheme, then he chucks me right in it by leaving *me* to write the associated programming, complete with a booklet of guidelines, and asks me to have it in his office within the next fortnight!'

I bent a sympathetic ear as we offered each other first use of the sugar bowl, but found it hard to ignore the boyish sniggers emanating from Mr Pickup, standing behind us in the queue.

Fortunately, Monica was too inflamed to notice, as she continued narrating her tale of woe: ' "Yes, Monica,' he says to me,' she imitated Mr Dick. ' "You can take over with the nuts and bolts now that we've got the scheme approved in principle' – as if he's doing me some kind of favour, for heaven's sake, after which he announces that he'll 'not be taking such a hands-on role in the project from now on.' And wait and bloody see,' she cursed loudly, 'whose name appears on the front cover of his precious sodding guidelines! Richard ruddy Dick, if I'm not mistaken! And another thing that really –'

She cut herself short, as Mr Dick bustled into the staffroom.

'Anyone seen George Crumley?' he queried in search of our principal geography teacher, before spotting him lounging in a corner. 'Ah, George,' he chirped brightly, 'time for a quick word? I wanted to see you about that record of achievement scheme I mentioned yesterday: d'you think we've got enough differentiation built into the achievement assessments?'

Mr Crumley's shoulders drooped even more visibly as he hauled himself from his armchair, sighed volubly, and walked slowly out of the staffroom with Mr Dick who, in sharp contrast, seemed extremely animated and enthusiastic about what appears to be yet another scheme.

Pickup looked triumphantly at me, but I turned my attention to comforting Monica instead. 'It's a shame, Monica,' I consoled her. 'I must say I thought Mr Dick's new pastoral care scheme showed he was taking a real *interest* in the kids. And if –'

'Hah!' Mr Pickup interrupted. 'The only person Dick Dick's interested in is himself and his promotion prospects! And as for kids – he wouldn't know one if he met one in the street!'

I still think he's being a little unfair . . .

Wednesday

With the exception of Rothesay O'Brien, I seem to have discovered a successful disciplinary measure with 2F: apparently, the threat of what I might say to their parents tomorrow evening about their classroom behaviour has filled them all with an unprecedented enthusiasm for work.

Sadly, Rothesay found herself unable to take a full part in our class debate on school uniform, having re-discovered the alternative pleasures involved in once more being able to make her nose bleed at will. It was an unpleasant distraction for the rest of the class.

Fiona Strangelove, with whom I share a team-teaching arrangement, has dismissed the girl as an attention-seeker and refuses to have anything to do with her. Personally, I think she needs a little genuine sympathy, and have tried to show a willingness to assist her in the matter of her nose-bleeds. I got through three clean handkerchiefs this afternoon alone.

I just hope her parents show up tomorow night, so I can get to the bottom of it all.

Thursday

Second year parents' evening tonight. It was not a great success.

I *had* been looking forward to a frank and detailed discussion with the parents of certain ill-disciplined members of 2F. Alas, the only parents who turned up were those whose offspring comprise the academic élite of the class, and with whom I could say little except to congratulate them on having such brilliant and enterprising children. It's always the same. Messrs McShane and McLeary, needless to say, had not turned up to debate the appalling behaviour of their

126

respective sons, and the only piece of truly interactive dialogue which arose on the night was, unfortunately, between the depute head and myself.

To explain, Mr Tod had armed himself with a little hand-bell to signal the conclusion of every eight-minute period, the length of time allocated to every interview tonight, and a timespan which allowed for two minutes of parental perambulation between the teachers with whom they had appointments. At the staff meeting preceding the parents' arrival, he had explained – exteremly rudely, in my opinion – that this was to avoid the 'usual log-jam which occurs outside the English department's room when Mr Simpson runs half an hour behind time'. I protested my innocence to him afterwards, not to mention my firm belief that parents have a perfect right to get a proper and fully-formed account of their children's progress, and that *I* could hardly help it if some parents were naturally talkative.

The man just grinned inanely, tinkled the bell in front of my nose, and told me that 'the man with the bell is the top man, Simpson.' How childish.

Surprisingly, many of the staff seemed to applaud the idea; personally, I found it an unwholesome irritation. I always feel it is necessary to put parents at their ease on such occasions, and like to spend the first few minutes of any such interview doing just this by discussing a few trivialities such as the weather and world affairs, before moving on to details of their child's classroom performance. Unfortunately, Mr Tod's ruddy bell persisted in moving everybody on with clockwork regularity, so that with most parents I was unable to do little more than discuss the adverse weather conditions pertaining at this time of year. Understandably, they seemed bewildered to be peremptorily thrust to their next interview by Mr Tod, having only discussed our respective difficulties in getting into work this morning, and without ever having had the chance to discuss their child's grading assessment and possible option choices for next year with me.

Except for Mrs O'Brien. Unfortunately, this sad little woman arrived for my last interview of the evening, already five minutes late, and proceeded to give me a blow-by-blow account of the reasons behind Rothesay's appalling behaviour. Just looking at the mother, to be honest, told me a great deal, for she seems to have had a hard life: a bedraggled little blonde figure in an ill-fitting black mini-skirt, she chain-smoked throughout our entire conversation, during which time she revealed that her daughter was, in fact, an unwanted child, the illegitimate product of a pre-marital jaunt to the Isle of Bute (hence her unusual forename). Alas, the natural father had not seen fit to provide for her, and Rothesay's emotional equilibrium, I discovered, had been further upset by the arrival of four subsequent step-fathers, none of whom had taken her into their affections. Worst of all, Mrs O'Brien's current husband, Andrew, had taken a particularly irrational dislike to the child based on a distant, alcohol-related incident on board a Caledonian-MacBrayne vessel in the very town of the girl's conception, the mere mention of whose name would invoke growls of bitter recollection and, occasionally, violent outbursts.

In circumstances like this, is it any wonder the girl is attention-seeking? Sometimes I wonder whether I'm a social worker or a teacher!

'Ah just hope ye can dae sumthin' wi' her,' Mrs O'Brien interrupted my reverie on the problem. 'That's how ah left the pub fur a wee bit, sose ah kid see hur guidey about hur.'

I endeavoured to explain that I was her daughter's English teacher, not her guidance one, but she had been distracted by some janitorial mutterings from Mr Crichton who, having switched off all other lights in the building, was standing at the classroom door, keys in hand, calling out, 'Cum in, numburr ten – yur time's up!'

'Oh ma Goad, is that the time?' shrieked Mrs O'Brien, looking at a plastic digital watch on her wrist. 'Ah'd better be gettin' back tae the pub!'

I lowered my eyes in what I hope she recognised as an indication of disapproval, and promised to try and help her daughter. Maybe I should give her some extra homework to keep her mind off her troubles.

'Now, Mistur Samson,' she mispronounced my name: 'Nut a wurd o' this tae anywan. If Andy wis tae hear whit ah'd said tae you the night, he'd -

I bade her good night, and assured her of my professional discretion in matters of confidentiality. Unfortunately, I was too late to catch the rest of the staff at the Pig and Whistle to tell them how Rothesay O'Brien got her name . . .

Friday

A pay-night celebration at the Pig and Whistle this afternoon after school, in which conviviality Mr Pickup and I were unusually joined by Monica Cunningham and George Crumley, both of them apparently intent upon drowning some sorrows, the nature of which soon became abundantly clear: Mr Dick's enthusiasm for new initiatives.

Mr Crumley, in particular, was infuriated by the large array of documents which have landed on his desk in what was supposed to be Mr Dick's record of achievement scheme, but which is rapidly showing signs of becoming Mr Crumley's record of achievement scheme – in all but name.

'Can't say I didn't warn you!' crowed Pickup. 'A whizz-kid, if ever I saw one. A different bandwagon for every week of the year, each one more ridiculous than the last, and each one guaranteed to send a snowstorm of paperwork flying round everyone's ears until he ends up with thirty different reports on his desk, all with his own precious name on the front as 'Project Co-ordinator', and all copied religiously to the education offices, ready for his next job interview.'

Actually, I'm beginning to agree with Pickup on this one: Mr Dick does seem to have a tremendous enthusiasm for the concept of delegation.

Anyway, I decided to change the subject and, while George and Monica were getting in the next round of drinks, quietly gave Pickup a confidential reprise of Mrs O'Brien's conversation with me last night. He seemed to find it all most amusing, despite my attempts to make him see a more serious side. Considering my request to him for secrecy, therefore, I was horrified to have him proclaim in a stentorian voice across the bar-room floor: 'Hey, George – d'ye hear what Simpson has to say about how Rothesay O'Brien got that ridiculous name?'

My discomfort was extended by his noisy, lager-enhanced retelling of the entire sorry saga, which concluded with the loud-mouthed observation that it was just as well that Mrs O'Brien hadn't been in Bognor or Skegness at the moment of her daughter's conception. However, things became *really* awkward when a small, fearsome blonde woman turned from the bar, and approached our table, recrimination in her sights.

'Haw, yoo!' Mrs O'Brien spat the accusation in my direction. 'So that's whit ye ca' keepin' a secret, eh? Sum bloody guidey *yoo* are!'

I endeavoured to explain, once again, that I was not her daughter's guidance teacher, but she brooked no interruption as she announced an intention to 'go fur ma man' and let him 'sort yees oot'.

Sensibly, we decided that discretion was the better part of valour, and left the Pig and Whistle as fast as courtesy would allow. George and Monica went home, but Mr Pickup suggested a continuation of our drinking session with a carry-out from the local off-sales. Foolishly – as it later transpired – I agreed.

February

Morris might have escaped the attentions of Mr O'Brien on that fateful night in The Pig and Whistle, but he still had to put up with the man's step-daughter in his classroom. Rothesay was, quite simply, the worst-behaved child he had ever come across, and her misdemeanours exceeded even the indiscretions of Tommy McShane and Alan McLeary. Ironically enough, as the months progressed she began to develop a degree of respect towards Morris, which any independent observer would have found hard to explain; perhaps, as one of nature's losers, she felt a certain affinity for him.

But this is to anticipate: in those first few weeks of their acquaintanceship, she kicked against the goad as no other child had done before. She was not just mischievous: the girl was a constant attention-seeker, and her demands upon Morris became extremely wearing. It meant that all of his time with 2F was devoted to dealing with this one child alone, while the few better pupils in the class, such as Janie Carswell, were frequently abandoned to their own devices and became consequently bored.

At least he was unlikely to be confronted with such accusations of negligence by Janie's father at the school board meetings: Morris had quietly resigned his position as staff representative at the beginning of February. He had missed several meetings this session and had become frankly bored with the seemingly endless and protracted discussions about the irrelevant minutiae of school life which the meetings usually produced. And anyway, it had become fairly obvious that, as an avenue for promotion, the school board was a dead end.

Of more likely benefit to his career, Morris reckoned, would be the continued cultivation of Mr Dick, most definitely a man who was going places. The scheme which he launched in February dealt with one of the more contentious issues of curriculum development: staff appraisal. Teachers have always had an ambivalent attitude to the prospect of staff appraisal: having admitted for years that of *course* there are bad teachers – as there are bad workers in any profession – they have nevertheless always displayed a marked reluctance to enter upon the practicalities of actually weeding such teachers out. However, the Government having taken a fairly dictatorial line on the need for implementing *some* kind of procedures for doing so, it had befallen the innovatory types such as Richard Dick to actually implement the programme, ensuring at all times that staff be made aware that appraisal – as the word implies – should include as much praise, as much positive comment, as it might (or might not) include constructive criticism.

At the end of February, however, Morris was having his mind turned towards the more immediately exciting – and disruptive – events surrounding Comic Relief Day. This day represented a regularly organised and laudable initiative of certain media personalities to gather financial aid for those in need by the simple expedient of encouraging as many people as possible to have a good time – and raise some cash in the process. As this, the third Comic Relief Day approached, however, it was becoming increasingly common for the associated celebrations, fund raising events – and even the wearing of the ubiquitous red plastic noses – to begin well in advance of the nominated date. As Morris recalls, Parkland High was no exception.

Monday

Comic Relief day approaches, some two weeks hence, but already the school seems to be inundated with red noses in preparation for the event. Personally, I think the whole affair has got completely out of control: I don't mind the occasional spot of light-hearted fun, especially when it's in a good cause, but the associated paraphernalia of charity events seems to go on for about a month before and after the day itself, with much consequent disruption to the working atmosphere (such as it is) within the classrooms of Parkland High.

Even some of the staff have taken to wearing these ridiculous red noses: indeed, Mr Pickup's garish plastic proboscis seems to have taken root to his face. I gather its constant appearance there is the result of a fund-raising challenge issued to him by some of the more attractive senior girls in the Ethics and Morals Module which he takes with the sixth year. They have sponsored him to wear it throughout each school day in the fortnight preceding Comic Relief day, whichever class he is teaching. Ever enthusiastic to make a good impression upon his 'young Lolitas', as he tastelessly describes them, his vanity had been unable to refuse the opportunity to win their acclaim.

'Yeh,' he leered when recounting the way the challenge had been oultined to him. 'April Morrison just fluttered her eyebrows, licked her lips suggestively, and said she'd always thought I was a really good sport. How could I refuse, old son?'

I still feel that putting Pickup in charge of an ethics class for sixth year girls is somewhat akin to leaving a wolf in charge of a hen-house, but decided instead to upbraid him on the less controversial matter of his ever-present red nose:

'It's quite appalling!' I complained. 'What kind of an impression d'you think you make on the junior classes – not to mention their parents – by lowering yourself to this kind of puerile humour?'

'Oh, come off it, Morris,' he slapped me on the back. 'It's just a bit of fun, and it's all in a good –'

'That's all very well,' I interrupted him. 'But it's demeaning and degrading to the profession. And it undermines the dignity of our calling.'

'Ah, stuff it,' rejoined my erstwhile friend. 'I haven't got time to argue, Simpson. Got a class to teach,' he chortled, a distant gleam in his eye. 'Sixth year ethics,' he grinned, after which he readjusted his plastic nose and headed towards Hut A56, a definite spring in his step.

Tuesday

More trouble with Rothesay O'Brien, the intensely disruptive new girl in class 2F. As her behaviour is so appalling, the school has been relieved of her presence for two days each week while she travels to Rockston special unit for behaviour remediation therapy.

In an economy-seeking measure aimed at lessening the transport costs involved in getting her there, the headmaster had suggested that Rothesay share a taxi with the sixth-year consortium pupils who travel to nearby Rockston High for their calculus classes. It is a relatively short journey, but a particularly serious bout of fighting broke out this morning between Rothesay and the senior pupils which resulted in the hospitalisation of one boy prefect – who was, ironically, trying to quell the disturbance in the back seat by turning round from the front – after the girl's teeth had drawn blood from his restraining wrist.

The staff were shocked to hear the news at lunchtime although, understandably, Mr Pickup's suggestion that the taxi-driver 'tie the little bitch to the roof-rack in future' did not meet with rectorial approval.

It has been decided to allocate a taxi for her sole use instead.

Wednesday

Richard Dick, our dynamic and youthful assistant head teacher, has started a staff appraisal scheme. The involvement of staff is to be purely voluntary, so Mr Dick was round the staffroom choosing his volunteers at morning break!

Unfortunately, the first person he singled out was George Crumley, principal teacher of geography:

'Sorry, Mr Dick,' answered Crumley between clenched teeth. 'I'm still too busy with the record of achievement scheme you started up with me last month. Or had you forgotten about it?' he asked sarcastically.

'No, no, not at all,' stammered Mr Dick. 'Very important scheme, of course, and I'm glad that we've got someone like you, George,' – Mr Crumley winced at the over-familiarity – 'to keep the ball rolling on that one. But we'll need to get going on this staff appraisal as soon as possible,' he continued, his eyes shifting constantly around the staffroom as he spoke to Crumley, frantically searching for some alternatives. They alighted, briefly, upon Monica Cunningham, before he recalled that particular lady's anger over his computer related pastoral support scheme which had, ultimately, landed in her lap instead of his.

Finally, his darting gaze came to rest upon Mr Major, his elderly equivalent in the school management structure, sitting quietly in a corner armchair, pipe clenched firmly between his teeth, coffee mug in hand and eyes serenely closed, enjoying a few minutes of inter-period relaxation.

'Mr Major,' he oozed over to the corner. 'Can I put you down for some staff appraisal, then? Setting a good example, and all that?'

A deathly hush fell upon the staffroom as everyone looked the other way, ears nevertheless straining to hear Bob Major's response. It was some time in coming, because Mr Dick had to wait to repeat the request until after Major had been fully roused from his slumbers.

'What!' he eventually laughed. 'Staff appraisal? Me? Oh come on, Dick: that's for upwardly mobile young thrusters like you, isn't it? Hardly very suitable for an AHT four years off retirement whose career's ground to an untimely end some fifteen years back!'

Unperturbed by Mr Major's blatant (if accurate) self-assessment, Mr Dick tried to outline the wider benefits of staff appraisal, in particular its potential for enhancing postive self-image and generating new ideas with otherwise moribund teachers.

It didn't wash. 'Sorry, old boy,' charmed Mr Major. 'Can't teach an old dog new tricks, y'know.' And that, it seemed, was that.

'Bloody appraisal,' whispered Pickup in my ear. 'I just hope that he doesn't ask *me* to go in for it next. I don't think I'd be able to keep a civil tongue in my head.'

Privately reflecting that it would be news to me that Pickup even *possessed* a civil tongue, I sought to reassure him that I thought his presence on a staff appraisal pilot would be one of Mr Dick's more unlikely requests.

'Oh?' he queried as he carefully positioned his plastic red nose around his nostrils once more, before setting out for his third year social education class. 'And why d'you think that?'

I avoided answering by looking down at my coffee mug and trying to conceal my continued disapproval of his foolish appearance. He really does look ridiculous.

Thursday

I have decided to volunteer for Mr Dick's staff appraisal pilot. Mr Pickup tried to warn me off it by repeating the litany of schemes initiated, and later abandoned, by our grasshopper assistant head, but I wasn't having any of it. It seems to me that Richard Dick is a man whose star is in the ascendant, and I have every intention of keeping in his good books.

'Up to you, Morris,' admitted Pickup when I rejected his advice as politely as possible. 'But don't say I didn't warn you. In fact,' he mused in afterthought, 'don't be too sure that Dick will even accept you, come to think of it.'

'Oh?' I asked, falling straight into his ill-concealed trap. 'And why shouldn't he?'

'Well, as far as I understand all this appraisal nonsense,' he explained, 'the whole point of it is to avoid saying anything *negative* about a teacher's performance and concentrate on identifying all of the *positive* things you can talk about and then building on them.'

Stupidly, I was still puzzled. 'Er . . . yes . . . ?'

'Well, where would he start with you, Morris? Name me something positive he could build upon. Where *could* he start?'

He burst into rude laughter, slapped me between the shoulder blades, and left the room. So much, once again, for friendship.

Friday

Much against my better judgement, I was today caught up in the ridiculous Comic Relief fever which is still sweeping the school.

April Morrison was to blame, I must admit: as Pickup has pointed out on numerous occasions, she really does have the most appealing eyes. However, things would never have been so ultimatey awful without the added involvement of Rothesay O'Brien.

To explain, the sixth year had aranged for a series of charity events to take place during today's specially extended lunch hour. Mr Pickup, for example, had agreed to organise a staff photograph (complete with red noses, copies to be sold at a later date), while Miss Tarbet had agreed to a sponsored face-painting session complete with attendant publicity from the local paper. Even Mr Dick had seen fit to join in the fun as one of the major targets at a Wet Sponge Throwing stall in the playground. Interestingly enough, the pupils in the queue for this attraction seemed frequently outnumbered by members of staff . . .

Faced with such frivolity, I found it difficult to reject April Morrison's alluringly couched suggestion that I 'join in the fun, sir.' She really is a most persuasive girl, because she managed to convince me that the temporary removal of just half of my recently acquired moustache in the aid of global charity would be a tremendously worthwhile gesture. 'Just for this afternoon, sir,' she breathed closely across my face, practically steaming up my glasses.

Before I'd had time to think up a proper excuse, the wretched girl had collected three sheets of sponsorship, a red plastic nose, and a photogapher from the *Parkland Gazette* to witness the event.

To be honest, it wasn't that bad, really: April provided me with a shaving kit, and a crowd of cheering pupils surrounded the event to applaud every razor stroke across the left-hand side of my upper lip; I reckon it should all have helped my credibility with some of the less academic charges under my direction. I even noticed that Rothesay O'Brien seemed to be finding it all a great joke, and the eventual sum of £178 raised for Comic Relief has actualy exceeded Pickup's expected intake for wearing his red nose throughout the fortnight.

The event was soured, alas, at the end of the afternoon when I came to remove the other half of my moustache lest I appear as ridiculous as Pickup. It was Rothesay O'Brien, I later discovered, who had been responsible for the surreptitious theft of the shaving eqipment – brush, soap and razor – so thoughtfuly provided for me by April Morrison, but it was long past five o'clock when Mr Crichton, the school janitor, telephoned me at home to announce the eventual discovery of this equipment in the 2nd year girls' toilet.

Before then, as you might imagine, I had endured the extremely embarrassing experience of a bus journey home, complete with half of a moustache adorning my right hand upper lip. I can still see the bus driver's face as I requested my fare, and I can still hear Pickup's voice repeating my own words as I left the staffroom in frustration at four o'clock: 'But you can't go home like that, Simpson. It's demeaning and degrading to the profession. And it undermines the dignity of our calling.'

I know what I'd have liked to have done with his red nose at that particular moment . . .

136

March

For all of the immediate distress and embarrassment which Comic Relief caused Morris Simpson, it did herald the continuation of a subtle alteration in the attitude of Rothesay O'Brien. Sensibly enough, Morris decided not to attempt issuing a punishment over the matter of the stolen razor and chose instead to ignore the matter altogether. Making distant recall of his educational psychology tutorials at teacher-training college, he recognised that bringing it up in her presence would constitute negative reinforcement of bad behaviour by giving the child the attention she so clearly desired. Difficult though it could sometimes be, he concentrated on praising the girl on the few occasions she merited it, and ignoring her for the rest of the time. It could be difficult – especially when she took it in mind to initiate a nose-bleed across her desk – but he made the attempt, and it seemed to pay dividends.

Otherwise, the beginning of the Easter holidays was to be preceded by the usual mad rush of last-minute preparation for SCE examinations – by some teachers at least – as well as the continuing disgust of Mr Ferguson at the length of time he was being made to wait before taking up his job-sharing arrangement.

Also of immediate interest to the Parkland staff was the most recent news concerning Morris's ex-principal teacher, Angela Bow-

137

man, yet one more victim of the education authority's restructuring programme. In retrospect, Morris realised, hers had been a case of 'a promotion too far', but news of her fall from grace still failed to deflect his own, renewed ambitions for career advancement. He just couldn't stop trying to impress people, as his diary for the last week of March will testify.

Monday

One up this morning on Ian Taylor, a senior teacher colleague from the English department. We were spending some of our departmental meeting discussing lesson units for the senior classes, and Taylor started wittering on about a series of lessons on 'register' which he was using with his fifth year. I sensed an opportunity to make an impression.

'Register?' I queried when he started crowing about the usefulness of his units. 'What's register when it's at home?'

He looked scornfully across at me. 'Tut, tut, Morris,' he chided sarcastically. 'Falling behind in the jargon stakes, aren't we?' I raised an eyebrow as he continued with disdain: 'I'd have thought that someone like *you* would know that register's the type of language appropriate to a given situation. I mean, really: an appreciation of a passage's register is *essential* if you're trying to prepare senior pupils for examinations – isn't that right, Simon?' he questioned Simon Young, our temporary principal teacher.

He was trapped! 'Oh, you mean *genre*,' I feigned surprise before Simon had time to reply. 'We don't talk about registers any more, Ian,' I explained solicitously. 'We talk about *genres* – don't we, Simon?'

'Er – well, yes, actually, Ian: Morris is correct,' Simon confirmed my statement with some embarrassment. 'Genre is the more preferred term these days – but I don't really think it matters terribly much,' he hurried to smoothe matters over.

'On the contrary, Simon,' I attempted to notch up a few more brownie points: 'I think you'll find that the exam board takes a dim view of the wrong terminology being used, and I was saying as much to my fifth year just the other day when introducing them to the concept of genres. In fact,' I elaborated, warming to my theme in front of the entire department, but especially the divine Fiona Strangelove, 'if you'd all care to take a look at the unit I've prepared on the language of estate agents, I think you'll find that it gives a pretty comprehensive explanation of what genre is all about. And it's certainly nothing to do,' I added pointedly in the direction of Ian Taylor, 'with anything as outmoded as registers!'

The effect of my triumphant claim was somewhat spoiled by Mr Major's sudden awakening from slumber.

'Registers?' he spluttered, rousing himself from his somnolent position. 'Registers, eh? Completely up to date, old boy! Got the summaries done yesterday!' Suddenly fully awake, he looked around, reminded himself of where he was, and went back to sleep instead.

Simon Young tactfully suggested we move on to the next item on the agenda, but I'm pleased to imagine that he'll have noticed my enthusiasm for curricular awareness. Ian Taylor didn't look so pleased, mind you, and I have to admit that Fiona looked positively bored. What can I do to impress the girl?

Tuesday

A late-night session of planned activity time, followed – by way of contrast – with a happy-hour visit to The Pig and Whistle with Mr Pickup. I spent some time attempting to enthuse him with the details of my estate-agent project with the fifth year, who really seem to be excited with the concept of utilisng genre in a variety of different contexts.

Sadly, Pickup seemed entirely disinterested, and in any case our discussion was cut short by the arrival at the bar of Mrs O'Brien, the unattractive and bedraggled mother of the even more unattractive and bedraggled second year girl, Rothesay O'Brien.

My heart sank to realise the woman's immediate proximity: for one awful moment I thought she was about to renew the verbal assault which had begun after the second year parents' night some weeks ago, when I inadvertently informed Mr Pickup of a number of confidential remarks she had made to me in the course of our discussion about the troubles which concerned her offspring.

Fortunately, she seemed in much better humour than on the night in question, a fact which was only partly attributable to the relatively minor quantity of alcohol she had consumed today; the rest of her cheerful disposition, it soon transpired, was apparently due to her ill-disciplined daughter's relative happiness at Parkland Community High School in comparison with the three other educational establishments into which she has been enrolled over the past eight months.

'Aye,' she rasped between drags at her cigarette. 'Ah've nivir seen Roathesay gettin' oan sae well at the schule.' I was about to question whether fourteen punishment exercises and three informal suspensions within eight weeks was such a wonderful record of achieve-

139

ment, but Mrs O'Brien was having none of it, preferring instead to recall my charitable efforts last month in removing half of my moustache for Comic Relief:

'And it's a' doon tae yoo, Misturr Samson,' she congratulated me, unfortunately mistaking my name. 'A' that stuff wi' the red nose an' the hauf-shaved musstach fur Coamic Rileef – Roathesay thoacht ye wir a screem – a reel big spoart!'

I was about to remind her that the larger part of my embarrassment during the day in question was entirely due to her child's gross tomfoolery with my shaving kit, but the woman was unstoppable, and proceeded to tell me of her common-law husband's enthusiasm for the curricular innovation displayed by the school: 'Andy's ferr pleased, Misturr Simpkins,' she informed me solicitously. 'Wants tae meet ye an' shek yur haund. Says anywan that can train that vicious wee bitch diserves a medal!' Never one to refuse a compliment – and fully recalling that at our last such meeting Mrs O'Brien had suggested that her husband would be more likely to shake my neck than my hand – I acquiesced in her judgement and acceped the praise with gladsome mind, though suggested we postpone our eventual meeting until a mutually convenient time.

'Aye, aye, right, Mr Sampson,' she forgot my name yet again, before repeating her misapprehension that I form part of the school's pastoral care structure by informing me that I was, in her eyes, 'the best guidey Roathesay's evir had!'

And maybe I am!

Wednesday

End of term draws near. The fifth year spent much of their double-period today demanding a final set of 'literature notes' with which to prepare for their Higher English examination next term. Of course, I have always resolutely refused to give them any such assistance in the form of examination cramming – despite their hotly-contested claims that I am the only member of the department to deny such co-operation.

Instead, we spent the time on a fairly entertaining diversion linked up with my unit on genres. The composition of several estate-agency style advertisements for some of the more dilapidated buildings around the Parkland area gave them all the chance to practise some creative writing as well as to appreciate just how much reading skill is necessary to discern the true meaning behind the glossy advertising language with which they are bombarded by today's media.

Even Craig Stewart, an easily distracted adolescent with whom I've had a few disagreements in the past, seemed to find the exercise quite amusing, for he provided a collection of 'For Sale' advertisements which made Parkland district sound like a Mediterranean holiday resort! At least it's stopped some of them worrying overmuch about their exams next month.

Thursday

Final day of term. Mr Ferguson's frustration over his unfulfilled request to 'job-share' his post as principal teacher of modern languages continues to be a source of confrontation with the regional staffing department. He has been informed that an advertisement for the position will be placed in the national press this month, though he seemed little pleased by the news this morning.

'My giddy aunt!' he exclaimed. 'They could save themselves a hell of a lot of cash if they'd simply send the details up to Pete Wilson over at Rockston High. I've told them twenty times over that it's the ideal solution, that we're both keen to work together, and that there's no *need* to advertise the post. Pete and I have got it all worked out already!'

I felt reluctant to repeat my secretly held belief that no staffing department in its right mind would allow such an important position to be shared by two of the region's most obstructive, argumentative and dyed-in-the-wool members of their employment pool, but kept my views to myself. In any case, I was much more interested in Mr Pickup's news that Angela Bowman has taken early retirement from her position as Adviser in English.

'Can you believe it?' he broadcast the revelation to an incredulous staffroom at morning break. 'Early retirement at forty-eight! God knows, I wish they'd offer it to me!'

Further enquiry revealed that Miss Bowman's departure has been hastened by the immediate implementation of a radically restructured advisorate aimed at ensuring a better quality of educational provision across the entire region. Miss Bowman has apparently claimed that her agreement to relinquish her post owed much to an altruistic desire to see this dynamic and innovatory service launched as soon as possible. Mr Pickup wondered if it also had something to do with the enormously generous financial handshake which she is reputed to have received, but I think he is being overly cynical, as usual.

For my own part, I can't help wondering if another window of opportunity might be opening up: Miss Bowman's departure, along with those of her advisorate colleagues in modern languages, social sujects, home economics, classics, mathematics, technical, religious education, and science means that – in Pickup's words – 'the advisers' offices are like a ghost town'. A post will be made available for a divisional adviser to cover all such responsibilities – and I know for a fact that Simon Young's got his eyes on it already. It all means possible movement in the department – and a possible promotion for me at the end of it all!

In fact, Mr Dick almost said as much to me at four o'clock as he reminded me of my recent promise to assist him in the launching of his staff appraisal project. 'Never know, Morris,' he whispered confidentially to me as we wished each other well for the Easter holidays. 'Play your cards right, make enough friends in the correct places –' and here he winked an eye, tapping his nose ever so slightly '– and who knows what could happen to your career from here on in?'

Who indeed? Hope springs eternal, as they say . . .

Friday

My hopes of a long lie-in were dashed by a 10am telephone call from the headmaster, of all people. I must say I took exception to having my holidays disturbed at such a premature stage, but Mr Ross seemed most agitated and asked me to make my way round to his house at the earliest conceivable opportunity.

'And bring a copy of the *Parkland Gazette* with you!' he barked down the telephone as I was about to hang up. I sensed from his tone that the invitation was not concerned with a discussion of my prospects for promotion – and so it proved.

Having dropped into the local newsagent on my way over, I was still leafing, bewildered, through the pages of the *Parkland Gazette* as I hurried up Mr Ross's garden path.

He was at the door to meet me, clad in overalls, and paint-brush in hand. Alas, the paint on his brush had long since hardened. As he explained to me, his intention of giving the house exterior an 'Easter coat' had been severely disrupted by an unending succession of telephone calls enquiring after the advertised sale of his own school! And what's more, he blamed *me* for the disturbance!

'There you are!' he jabbed a finger at the property pages of our local newspaper. 'Look at that!'

It was an impressive advertisement, I had to admit, and showed a keen appreciation of estate-agency wiles:

FOR SALE: New to the market! This impressive baronial mansion has bright, generously proportioned accommodation comprising 42 rooms, incl. four large public rooms, massive dining hall, eight bathrooms, plus extensive grounds and outbuildings. Must be viewed! Close to all amenities. In need of major internal and external renovation, as reflected in price. Telephone Parkland (0589) 867950 Ref: M. Simpson.

The telephone number, needless to say, belonged to Mr Ross. The property described, needless to say, bore close resemblance to Parkland High School. And – at an asking price of just over two hundred thousand pounds – Mr Ross's telephone had understandably been besieged since nine o'clock by an endless stream of calls from entrepreneurial property developers enquiring about the possibility of hotel and/or studio flat conversions. Indeed, just prior to my arrival, he had fielded a call from an extended family unit with an urgent desire for granny-flat accommodation! My stomach churned as he demanded an explanation over the appearance of my name in the offending advertisement.

Sensing an ill-timed attempt at an April Fool prank from my fifth year, I muttered something about my exercises on genre and made mental note to seek out Craig Stewart on the first day back of the summer term.

At this point, Mr Ross became very red, very angry, and was, I sensed, just about to say something he might have regretted when the telephone rang once again.

'Bloody hell!' he swore at me. 'Hold this, Simpson!' he thrust a paint-encrusted brush into my hand and stormed back inside the house, leaving me alone at the doorstep.

'Maybe you should go ex-directory?' I suggested tentatively after his retreating footsteps. In retrospect, it was probably just as well that he didn't hear me.

April

The Easter holidays came, and went, and quickly. Morris's return to school for the summer term was not made any easier by the headmaster's understandable displeasure at having his school put up for sale – an auction, so to speak, for which he still held Morris personally responsible. Morris just hoped that Mr Dick would put in a good word for him here and there, especially if the plans for staff appraisal worked out as he hoped they would. This year, he thought, *must* be the year for promotion, even if it was only on a temporary basis.

Temporary promoted posts were, in fact, in some abundance at Parkland Community High that summer term. Apart from Simon Young's apparently everlasting appointment as acting principal teacher (27 months and still counting), there was a plethora of other staff who found themselves 'acting up' – in a professional sense, that is. Frank Parker, for example, was still to be accorded the status of a permanently appointed APT guidance, while poor Martin Henderson was still holding the history fort during Miss Denver's second maternity leave, due to conclude just in time for the summer holidays to begin. And – possibly a mixed blessing – he had just learned that a student history teacher had been allocated Parkland High as his

144

final teaching practice of the year; at least his presence would allow for class cover during the manifold occasions when Martin was being called away for an ever-increasing diet of in-service courses – some of which were proving decidedly less useful than others, as Morris's diary for April will reveal.

Otherwise, this month's record of events finds Morris encountering the same endless rounds of classroom indiscipline which had made his professorial life so difficult from the outset. The further he went in his teaching career, the more impatient he found himself with the outright disobedience proclaimed by some of his pupils – especially those like Tommy McShane, who seemed to take a perverse delight in challenging his authority just for the *sake* of it . . .

Monday

Tommy McShane arrived in class this afternoon, sporting a large, decorative earring adorned with sharp spikes, the whole of it dangling fearsomely from his right lobe. I told him to remove it at once:

'You look ridiculous, McShane!' I condemned him. 'Apart from displaying a complete disregard for the school's rules on uniform, a piece of weaponry like *that* one is likely to cause severe injury to anyone unlucky enough to come within touching distance of you.'

For a moment I thought he was about to flaunt my authority, because he gave me a sullen, evil look but – with an extremely bad grace – he eventually launched himself into a protracted wrestling session with the jewellery in question, after which removal he placed it on the front of his desk, challenging me to question its presence there.

I ignored it and continued with the lesson.

Tuesday

A drink with Mr Pickup and Martin Henderson (acting principal teacher of history) at four o'clock, during which session Martin informed us that he was looking forward to the arrival of another pair of hands in the department tomorrow: Michael Pratt has apparently *chosen* to come to Parkland High for the last teaching practice of his course – maybe the lad has a masochistic streak about him!

The other main happy-hour topic of conversation was Martin's explanation behind his absence from school yesterday: apparently, he had been forced to attend a wearisome in-service course concerned with finalising syllabus arrangements for the revised Higher grade examination in history.

'Honestly!' he complained. 'Talk about the blind leading the blind: I'd bet even-money that most of that course was cobbled together on Sunday afternoon, about 24 hours before we met up. Nobody seemed to have a bloody *clue* about what was going on, least of all the organisers. We needed three 'brainstorming sessions' to fill up the morning, and the afternoon was down to a question-and-answer session on support materials for option selection .'

Oh?' I enquired briefly of him, recalling the immense mountains of paper which had threatened to bury Martin's department from sight during the early days of Standard grade. 'I hope they're going to be a little more circumspect in the amount of worksheets they send out this time.'

'That's exactly it!' Martin laughed in recollection. 'Somebody else asked that as well. The development officer looked quite smug: turned round and said that they'd all learned their lessons from the Standard grade worksheets, thank-you very much. Recognised they'd been a little over-ambitious and that sometimes the quality of the materials had compared unfavourably with the quantity. 'Really,' he explained to us, 'we gave you all far too much stuff last time round,' before going on to assure us that they wouldn't make the same mistake with the Higher.' Martin's mind wandered back to the development office's explanation, clearly savouring the moment.

'So what are they giving you this time?' demanded Mr Pickup.

'Nothing.'

'What?'

'Nothing. That's what the man said. Zero. Sod all. You're on your own, pal.' Martin stopped laughing, and became serious, even bitter. 'Once more unto the breach, dear friends, seems to be the attitude. Prepare yourselves – and your classes – for a completely new exam – but don't expect us to provide the materials to help you teach it.'

'That's terrible,' I complained. 'Just what are these people getting *paid* for?'

'Search me,' replied Martin. 'Organising courses, I suppose.'

Wednesday

Terrible news! Two years after the successful conclusion to Mr Major's 'Save Our School' campaign, the whole messy issue has raised its head again!

Having thought our future secure, it was a source of great distress to learn from the *Parkland Gazette* this morning that the region is planning yet another review of school capacities, and that the possible merger of Parkland and Rockston High Schools is high on the list of priorities once more. Mr Ross was furious, and contacted the regional offices straight away – as Mrs Thomson from the office, listening into his conversation from the switchboard, informed us later:

'Yes – that's right,' she confirmed. 'Absolutely steaming mad – asked if they could perhaps tell him why they'd considered it necessary to inform the local press they were planning to close the school before they'd had the courtesy to inform the headmaster?'

'But we *did* tell you!' the lady at the other end of the line had, apparently, protested. 'We posted out the details last month. And you never *usually* reply to our correspondence before five weeks are up, so we could hardly be expected to know you hadn't got it this time, could we?'

'Harrumph!' Mr Ross had parried unsuccessfully. 'Well, how did you send it, then? By carrier pigeon?'

'No, no,' she assured him. 'By the internal mail system.'

'Hah! Say no more!' Mr Ross scorched in revenge before hanging up without further discussion. Mrs Thomson tells us that he's never been tremendously impressed by the efficiency of the regional offices.

Certainly, whatever happened to the original documentation outlining the region's plans, it looks as if we've got another fight on our hands at Parkland Community High. I just hope we've got the stomach for it second time around.

Thursday

Consternation still abounds over our possible merger with Rockston and the fight to avoid it, but I had my own little personal battle to conduct this morning with Tommy McShane. The boy has reverted to wearing an earring, albeit a smaller gold affair this time, in direct contravention of my instructions earlier this week.

Once again, he glared at me with the most appallingly disrespectful expression on his face when I demanded its removal and told him it made him look more like a girl than a boy. I glared back, and he returned my look with the steeliest of sullen, disobedient and downright evil gazes. The silence – and the tension – mounted until it became almost unbearable. I began to be concerned lest he stare me out, but I held my ground for several minutes until, eventually, I was rescued by one of his classmates: Rothesay O'Brien, of all people.

'Simpy's right, McShane,' she broke the tensely-held silence, and bellowed across the classroom. 'Ye look a right fuckin' pansy! Get the bluddy thing aff – now!'

I refrained from criticising her mode of expression lest I weaken my case with McShane. He, in turn, had met his match. Few members of 2F would take on Rothesay O'Brien in open conflict, and McShane knew his limitations. Slowly, and still with a very bad grace, he averted his eyes and removed the offending article:

'It's no ferr,' he muttered beneath his breath. 'That new teechur's goat wan oan.'

I couldn't decide what he meant by that – we haven't *got* a new teacher, and if we did, he certainly wouldn't be wearing an earring, but I chose not to continue the discussion. The exchange had left me a little shaken, not to mention bewildered by the intervention of Rothesay O'Brien, normally the most disobedient child in the class. It's certainly true that I've been following a policy of positive reinforcement with the girl, in line with the suggestion of her educational psychologist, but I hadn't expected her co-operation and wholesome support as quickly as this.

Maybe she just likes me for myself, of course, as her mother so recently assured me. It would be nice to think that *somebody* did.

Friday

Mr Dick's staff appraisal project looks to have been postponed for a few weeks. He explained swiftly to me this morning that he was currently working on a whole-school policy document on developing anti-racist education in Parkland High, and that its implementation was to be even swifter than the staff appraisal plan.

'But I haven't forgotten your offer to help out with the pilot, Morris,' he assured me, 'and I'm very grateful to you.'

We made a tentative agreement to take up the reins again in a few weeks: actually, I'm only too pleased to discover he feels himself to be in my debt – he looks like being a useful man to know.

My other discovery this morning was the revelation, just before lunch, that Tommy McShane had actually been telling the truth about the jewellery which bedecks the left ear of one of my colleagues. A semi-colleague, I suppose, because the adornment in question belongs to Michael Pratt, the history student who is working with Martin Henderson, and whom I encountered for the first time today

To be honest, I have never seen such a sight: I almost turfed him out of the staffroom this morning under the mistaken impression that he was there to empty the bins! He sported jeans, long blonde hair with a pony-tail, an open-necked shirt with a wide-eyed look to match – and the aforementioned earring to boot! If this is the sort of slovenly teacher that the colleges are turning out today, then it's little wonder that the pupils are as appallingly ill-mannered as they are.

I decided to give him a few words of tactfuly-addressed advice about professional appearance, which he seemed to take in good spirit – at first.

'Thanks. Oh, thanks very much, Mr . . . er?' he responded to my initial suggestions.

'Simpson. Morris Simpson.'

'Right. Thanks. I'll bear that in mind about the tie.'

'Well, it *would* help to create a better impression, and –'

'Yes, you're quite right,' he assured me, a slight grin creeping around his lips. 'And I'll check out the wherabouts of my three-piece suit at the same time. And maybe my dinner jacket as well?'

I think he was being sarcastic, but decided to press on regardless: 'And I thought maybe I should warn you in avance not to be upset or offended if any of the kids make jokes about your surname.'

'Oh?' he appeared the picture of innocence 'Why should they?'

'Well, Pratt's got some..uh.. fairly obvious connotations, and kids can be pretty cruel, sometimes, and..er..' I tailed off miserably.

'Well, nobody's made fun of it in my *previous* teaching practices, Mr Morris,' he explained, the picture of innocent surprise, and accidentally mistaking my name. I think.

'Oh. Well,' I flustered. 'Um. Well, never mind that just now, but possibly they might, and..um..,' I continued, searching desperately for more certain ground, 'er, possibly you should..um..consider leaving off . . .'

'Yes . . . ?' he raised his eyebrows.

I looked pointedly at his earring, but he didn't quite seem to pick me up on it, so I had to explain myself more bluntly. 'Well, quite frankly, Martin, a piece of jewellery like that on your ear's going to lead some of the kids to start questioning your . . . eh . . .'

'Yes?' he waited for me to finish. He wasn't helping matters at all.

'Your..um.. y'know,' I whispered confidentially. 'Your sexual *leanings*.'

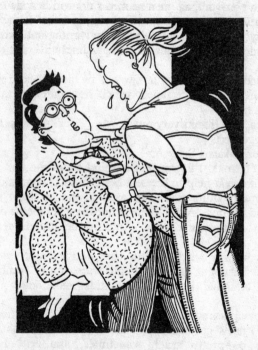

That did it all right. I have seldom been subjected to such a torrent of personal abuse as that which followed. In it, the young Mr Pratt ventured to suggest, among other things, that he considered me to be an 'interfering, suspicious, small-minded and petty little fishwife'. The cheek of it! He also suggested that I keep any future such words of advice which I might wish to impart strictly to myself; otherwise,

150

he advised me, he would have little alternative other than to ram his tightly clenched fist as far down my throat as the width of his arm would allow! And finally, in a summary display of rudeness, he advised me that as far as his sexual proclivities were concerned it would be very unwise of me to initiate *any* rumours concerning this area of his private life; if I did, he maintained, I would find myself – and here he looked around for inspiration before grabbing hold of a nearby window-pole – 'with half of this pole thrust up your rear-end and the other half planted in the ornamental garden just outside the art department!'

I drew myself back in amazement. Speechless with shock, I watched him stride purposefully over to the corner where Fiona Strangelove was sitting, an enormous grin on her face. Hurriedly, she jumped up to meet him, whispered something conspiratorial in his ear and pecked him on the cheek before they walked arm in arm out of the staffroom – heading, I was later told, for a bar-lunch. Together. And alone.

Maybe I misjudged him.

May

As the senior pupils finally drifted away from regular classroom attendance to avail themselves of study-leave for their SCE examinations, the usual host of alternative staffroom attractions was initiated at Parkland High.

Mr Major again organised the annual Scrabble championship, Miss Tarbet once more inaugurated the spring-term knitting bee, and Mr Pickup finally launched himself into a spring-clean of Hut A56. Meanwhile, those members of staff not involved in any of the foregoing activities could usually be found in the TV room catching up on the latest frames from the world professional snooker championship, always so thoughtfully scheduled by the snooker and television authorities for a school term which is more generous than others in its provision of pupil non-contact time. Aside from worry over the proposed school merger, then, the four weeks of May provided a welcome respite for the teachers of Parkland High, a chance to relax from the daily troubles which beset them when faced with a full teaching timetable as well as the usual host of alternative professional demands.

Mr Dick, of course, was different. He did not appear to need much relaxation from educational demands and, conversely, he had little interest in the proposed merger of Rockston with Parkland

High; after all, he had little intention of remaining in Parkland for any longer than it took to gain his next promotion. However, he *was* still interested in enhancing his professional reputation by whatever means he could. In this – if in nothing else – Richard Dick and Morris Simpson had identical concerns. Simpson's diary for May takes up the story.

Monday

Mr Dick has at last got around to arranging my pilot appraisal interview, although I was disappointed to learn that the discussion in question would be drastically curtailed from the 60 or so minutes which I understood to be the recommended timespan for such a session.

'No, no, Morris,' he told me at morning break. 'Pop round to my office for about 15 minutes after lunch tomorrow – that should be long enough.'

'Will it?' I queried him. 'I've spent quite a bit of time boning up on the guidelines for these appraisals, and I can't imagine how we'll get through all of the required process steps in 15 minutes.'

'Nonsense, nonsense,' he assured me. 'And anyway: I've got my anti-racist policy document to have finished by Wednesday, so we might not even have *that* long.'

I must say, I don't know how he expects to explore the depths of my job motivation in quarter of an hour, but I held my tongue: I still feel that keeping on the right side of Richard Dick could be of paramount importance to my future career. Certainly, I hope to gain his approval for my last-minute decision to apply for the temporary (temporary) post which has become available due to Frank Parker's secondment from his own 'acting' appointment as APT guidance. He has gone away for a year to develop a pastoral care structure for single-parent children in schools which are situated in disadvantaged catchment zones, or Areas of Priority Treatment as they are more properly known.

Indeed, as I wittily remarked to Mr Pickup before taking my application form along to the office this afternoon: 'Just think, Pickup: I could be a temporary APT for a temporary APT who's just been temporarily seconded to look after an APT!'

'Very droll, Simpson,' he frowned, before turning to his news-paper again. The man has no sense of humour.

Tuesday

My appraisal interview was a bit of an anti-climax, as well as being extremely unsettling. Awash with trepidation, but extremely well-prepared, I knocked on Mr Dick's door just after lunch as arranged, and he bade me enter.

'Yes? What d'you want?' he raised his head from an immense collection of paperwork – the outlines of his anti-racism document, as I later discovered.

'Um . . . my appraisal interview..?' I hesitated.

'Blast!' he struck his forehead. 'Forgot all about it, Morris. Never mind. Come in, come in and sit down,' he welcomed me, hastily rummaging through several drawers of his desk to locate what later transpired to be his draft instructions for carrying out an appraisal interview.

Things went from bad to worse. Far from putting me at my ease with a cup of coffee and a friendly, introductory chat, as I had been led to believe would happen, he remained enthroned on his high-backed leather swivel chair, from which vantage point he gazed over at me in the corner of the room, sunk into the depths of an ancient armchair which appeared to have lost most of its stuffing, my arms awkwardly raised at an extremely uncomfortable angle to remain on the chair-sides.

Then – contrary to all of the recommended instructions for breaking the ice and encouraging me to open out with my own thoughts of positive self-image (a part of the appraisal to which I was secretly looking forward) – Mr Dick insisted on outlining the litany of disasters which he understood my career to have mainly comprised up until this point. Having completed a diatribe which lasted some several minutes, and which recalled various unpleasant memories of pupil indiscipline, parental complaints and organisational chaos which he claimed I had initiated, he eventually stopped to draw breath.

This wasn't following the pattern I had expected, but I determined to turn the interview around to a more laudatory theme.

'Well, actually, Mr Dick, it hasn't been *all* gloom and doom, you know,' I started.

'No?' he raised his eyebrows.

'No. And I thought the whole point of these appraisals was to give me the chance to outline where I thought I'd *succeeded* in my career, where I thought I'd made a real *go* of it?'

He began to snigger rudely, but then drew himself up. 'Yes, yes – you're quite right, Morris –'

'Ah good,' I said. 'Well, I'd like to start by –'

'– but we haven't got time for all of that crap, I'm afraid, so I've got *this* ready for you to sign.' And so saying, he withdrew an appraisal form from his set of guidelines which, to my absolute horror, was *already completed*!

'As they say on TV, here's one I made earlier,' he smiled across at me. I was dumbfounded. We were supposed to arrive at an appraisal of my qualities *together*: this was contrary to all of the guidelines concerning staff appraisal which I had read, and if it contained even half of the outrageous things of which he had just accused me, then my career would be finished. The man must have seen my concern.

'Don't worry, Morris. It reads O.K. Here – take a look,' he handed me the appraisal sheet.

I took a few minutes to glance over what Mr Dick had already written, and found myself wondering if this was the same person he had just been describing some five minutes earlier. True, his document could hardly be considered a eulogy of congratulation, but neither could it be classed as a fearsome indictment of my teaching skills. Two phrases of rather damning faint praise which kept cropping up in his assessments of me were 'amiable' and 'well-intentioned', but I was certainly gratified to realise that the man had shown a willingness to highlight my better qualities rather than my worst – even to the extent of supporting my application for a temporary promoted post in the guidance sector of the school.

'Hell's teeth, Morris – why not?' he challenged me. 'You couldn't make more of a cock-up than the present lot in this place, and I'm very grateful to you for your assistance in this staff appraisal pilot. Now, if you'll just sign here . . .'

He held a pen quickly across the desk as I struggled to get out of the armchair.

'Thanks very much,' he continued. 'Now, I'll have to get back to work, if you don't mind.' Too bewildered for further discussion, and uncertain lest he change his mind, I signed as quickly as I could and left his room with a spring in my step, as well as – for the first time in my career – a real *optimism* about my chances for promotion.

Wednesday

A cloud of uncertainty still hangs over the school concerning our possible merger with Rockston High, but the region seems to be playing its cards very close to its chest. Mr Pickup thinks they will keep quiet about the final decision to close Parkland until after the summer holidays begin, after which, he claims, 'they could fill in this dump with solid concrete, and nobody'd be any the wiser until next August. And who'd even miss us then, to be honest?'

I found it difficult to support his contention, but was eager to move the discussion on to my bewildering pilot appraisal yesterday. Here again, it was impossible to surprise the man:

'But Morris,' he explained patiently to me. 'He's not *bothered* what he puts on your appraisal form.'

'No?'

'No. Never has been. The only thing that Dick Dick ever wanted from this was another line to add to his *c.v.* for the next job application: now he can say that he's 'assisted in implementation of staff appraisal pilot scheme'. And all he needed for *that* to happen was a willing volunteer to sign a name at the bottom of his own appraisal.'

'Does that mean he doesn't *really* think I've got a good chance of promotion, then?'

'Shouldn't think he's bothered, quite frankly. Except you've helped *him* on his way, so it's fairly likely that he'll repay the favour, even if he doesn't think you deserve it. Honour among thieves, they call it, Morris.'

I protested my innocence of such a Machiavellian scheme, but Pickup didn't seem to think there was anything wrong with the notion in the first place.

'It's quite simple, Morris,' he advised me as we went to our respective classes. 'You play ball with him, and he'll scratch yours . . .'

I think he got his metaphors rather mixed, but I know what he meant. And who knows? He could be right.

Thursday

Mr Dick's new anti-racist policy document was delivered to all staff-rooms today, and a weighty tome it looks. Personally, I couldn't face the prospect of ploughing through its 140 pages, but Michael Pratt (our bohemian history student with pony-tail and earring to match) spent most of the afternoon poring over its contents, nodding animatedly in approval all the while. I gather the lad's been involved heavily in this sort of thing at college – the enthusiasm of youth, I suppose – but decided not to involve myself in a discussion of anti-racist guidelines with him.

We didn't hit it off terribly well last month, to be honest, and

I've been avoiding him ever since. Anyway, he also seems to have developed a strong bond of affection towards Fiona Strangelove, for whom I still hold a burning candle myself. Alas, it looks likely to be extinguished pretty soon, the way she and Michael were giggling in a corner together at four o'clock.

Friday

It's amazing! In all the time I've been at Parkland we've never had the slightest hint of racism or associated troubles. Yet here we are – only 24 hours after Mr Dick has delivered a policy document on the subject – and the staff has been split by a particularly bitter argument on the subject!

It all started when Mr Pickup was making derisory comments about the bulk of the aforementioned document at morning break.

'Load of crap!' he dismissed it sweepingly, before making great play of inserting a copy beneath the corner leg of an old blackboard we have in a corner of the staffroom. 'There!' he proclaimed triumphantly. 'Found a use for it at last – that blackboard's been wobbly for months!'

'*If* you don't mind, Mr Pickup,' lisped Michael Pratt, bending down to retrieve the volume. 'I was just going to have another look at this. And it's a *chalk*board, not a blackboard.'

'Eh?' Pickup looked surprised.

'I said it's a *chalk*board. Blackboard is a racist term,' Michael explained impatiently, '– as you'd know full well if you bothered to read your own school's guidelines!'

'Sorry, Michael,' Pickup apologised with unusual tact. 'Hadn't realised I was being offensive.' Turning away from him, he nevertheless pursed his lips at me and gently slapped his own wrist before deliberately wobbling the blackboard again. Michael looked up sharply from his reading, and there was an awkward moment. It passed, but there was a tense atmosphere about the staffroom for the rest of the interval.

Unfortunately, the tension had grown worse by the afternoon break. To begin with, Mr Pickup had cheerfully returned from his Friday lunchtime libation at The Pig and Whistle to sober himself up with a cup of coffee. Michael, standing by the urn as Pickup approached, had politely offered to make amends for their earlier tiff by 'being mother', so to speak.

'With milk or without, Mr Pickup?' he asked.

'Oh – white, please, Michael,' answered Pickup.

'With milk – or without?' repeated Michael sharply.

'White please, I said, Michael,' repeated Pickup in turn.

Michael frowned. 'In that case, I'd prefer for you to ask for it with milk, Mr Pickup.'

'What on earth *for*?' questioned Pickup, before a dawn of comprehension cleared his face, followed swiftly by an expression of extreme irritation. 'Oh, for God's sake, Pratt, don't be ridiculous!'

Michael stood his ground; ' "Black" and "white" are racist terms, Mr Pickup – there's no getting away from it: and comments, and attitudes, like yours are exactly the kind of thing which Mr Dick wishes to be recorded in the school's record of racist incidents.'

'And it's over-zealous little prats like *you*,' declaimed Pickup -pardoning the personal reference – 'who get racism a bad name! You *cause* the trouble instead of preventing it!' he complained loudly. 'Aw, stuff the coffee!' he concluded angrily. 'I've got a class to teach!' With which he stormed out of the staffroom.

By the time the afternoon interval came round you could have cut the atmosphere with a knife. Everyone was scared to open their mouths lest Michael Pratt misinterpret their remarks. Everyone except Pickup, that is. An innocent abroad, he seemed oblivious to the consequences when he barged into the staffroom halfway through the interval:

'Right then!' he enquired of the assembled company. 'Pay night celebrations tonight: anyone fancy joining me for a Chinkie . . . ?'

Michael Pratt was up off his seat like a scalded cat. Furiously, he brushed past Pickup – 'I presume your invitation refers to a Chinese meal, Mr Pickup?' he scorched – and headed straight for the office of Richard Dick, there to place on record his indignation at such inflammatory terminology. He appeared to have the support of several members of staff, Fiona Strangelove included.

'Oh my God,' exclaimed Pickup. 'That'll be *my* name in the wog-log, I suppose.'

It was hardly a very respectful term for Mr Dick's record-book of racist incidents, and I chastised Pickup later for such an indelicate remark. Nevertheless, I confess to a certain sympathy for the base of his complaint. We've certainly never had any racism at Parkland before now . . .

More cheerfully, from my own point of view at least, was the news which greeted me as I left the building at four o'clock. I had just walked past Mr Dick's office when he called out to me.

I turned back and found him engaged in the company of Michael Pratt, a large tome in front of them – the racist incident log, I presumed – the first page of which comprised a palimpsest of virgin ruled paper, on whose top line he had just begun to inscribe the name of 'D. Pickup'.

'Just to let you know you're on the short-leet for Frank Parker's guidance job. O.K?' – and here he tapped the side of his nose gently with his finger – 'Say no more, eh?'

I swallowed hard, mumbled some words of gratitude and stumbled backwards out of his office. Unfortunately, I caught my footing on a large collection of policy documents which were at the corner of the entrance, and ended up spread-eagled backwards in the corridor. Mr Dick looked disbelievingly over his desk as I began to pick myself up in undignified confusion.

'The interview's next month, Morris,' he sighed loudly. And then, in a heartfelt plea of supplication, he urged: 'Try and create a good impression, will you? Just for once. Eh . . . ?'

I said I would. And I shall.

June

It had been a long wait – seven years, to be precise – but at last Morris Simpson stood on the threshold of promotion. During the month of June he could understandably think of little else other than his forthcoming interview, scheduled for the penultimate day of the session.

Other members of staff still had other concerns, as will become apparent in Simpson's diary for the month, but on this one interview depended the happiness – or otherwise – of his entire summer holiday, not to mention his future career. It was to be a momentous week, and as this – his third volume of educational memoirs – draws to a rapid conclusion, it as well to let Simpson take up the story as quickly as possible.

Monday

Frantic preparations for my interview on Thursday have made this last week of the session a good deal more hectic than usual. I've been swotting up on all of the guidance manuals I could lay my hands on, and am determined to fulfil the faith shown in me by our AHT Richard Dick: it was he who supported my application for a temporary APT post in the school's guidance team – in the face of strong opposition, I have since learned, from the headmaster – and I don't want to let him down.

Everyone has been very kind in wishing me luck for the big occasion, though some have been a little more disbelieving than others on hearing that I had attained the short-leet. In particular, Fiona Strangelove could hardly conceal her scorn last month, and eventually embarrassed me no end by staggering to a corner of the staffroom to pass on what she obviously considered to be the hilarious news to her disreputable boyfriend, Michael Pratt (our history student). At least *he's* out of the way now, having taken his ridiculous pony-tail and earring back to college for the last three weeks of term. Unfortunately, his legacy still remains, firstly in the form of Mr Dick's racist incident log-book which has three pages completed already (though none since Pratt left, interestingly enough), and secondly in the form of an extremely distanced Fiona Strangelove. The girl – once such an avid, professional teacher – seems to have become easily distracted, almost to the point of losing interest in the job altogether.

Pickup thinks she's pining for Pratt, and I suspect he could be right; anyway, I've written myself out of the frame with regard to the possibility of ever winning the girl's affections. I have decided instead to dedicate my life anew to education and to the children beneath my care. Well, that's what I'm planning on saying at my interview at any rate!

Tuesday

Miss Denver returned from her second successive maternity leave in two years today, just in time to take up full position as principal teacher of history (with correspondingly full pay, of course) before the holidays begin.

'How does she do it?' questioned Pickup at morning break. 'That's two years on the trot that she's had almost an entire school session off for maternity leave, yet still managed to get back in time for a fully paid summer holiday. How does she do it?' he repeated.

I decided that this wasn't a suitable occasion – nor Pickup a suitable partner in conversation – to engage in a discussion on the mysteries of female ovulation cycles, and chose instead to ask how Martin Henderson, Miss Denver's long-suffering temporary replacement, had taken the news of his second successive summer on reduced pay, despite having once again done all of his superior's work for the previous eight months.

'Unavailable for comment,' Pickup told me, 'although I think he intends having a quiet word with Sandra Denver's boyfriend before long. Either that, or he plans to put some bromide in his tea –'

Wednesday

More disharmony over holiday pay, this time from our principal teacher of modern languages: Mr Ferguson has at long last – seven months after his original request – had news of his job-sharing application. However, his intital pleasure upon receiving the news from the staffing department was soon transformed to violent anger.

'That's great,' he had responded to the telephone call which first alerted him to news of the new appointment. 'So when will Mr Wilson be taking up the other half of the job, then?'

His reddening hue soon informed the rest of us, innocently pretending not to be listening, that the potential job-sharer was not, indeed, to be Ferguson's old pal Peter Wilson from Rockston: he, it soon transpired, has been granted early retirement on the grounds of mental ill-health.

'So who's coming to share with me, then?' enquired Ferguson, already clearly irritated that Peter Wilson had so obviously succeeded in an early retirement application where he had failed. His face, upon hearing the answer, was a picture to behold.

'WHAT?' he bellowed down the 'phone. 'Certainly not! No way, as they say, am I sharing my promoted post with *that* little madam! Think again! And let me know when you've come up with something better than a jumped-up firecracker!' he concluded, slamming down the telephone.

Alas for Mr Ferguson, this was not the end of the matter. His explanation to us that the 'staffing department had tried to foist bloody Francoise Leleu' on to him as a job-sharer was interrupted by the impatient summons of the telephone bell: the staffing department once again, this time to explain sharply to Mr Ferguson that – as Mrs Leleu was the only applicant misguided enough to want to share a post with him – the appointment had been taken out of their hands. She would be taking up post by the end of this week.

'What!' gasped Ferguson. 'But she can't. I'd go on to half pay for the holidays – I mean, sorry, um, the..um.. department's not ready for her yet. How can it be? I mean. We haven't worked out the arrangements yet. It's all too sudden. Why not leave it till August? Eh?'

It was all to no avail. Francoise Leleu, a native French speaker, is due to join the school on Thursday; having just returned from a secondment as staff development officer, she had apparently antici-pated domestic difficulties with her four children in having to return to a job which would no longer be so flexible in its working hours, hence her application to job-share. Nevertheless, she is – by all accounts – a very dynamic and enthusiastic young teacher who has developed several exciting new schemes of work in the past.

The very antithesis, in fact, of Jack Ferguson. No wonder he looked worried.

Thursday

Interview day. As I write, I look back on an afternoon which I hope will prove to be a turning point in my career, a new educational dawn in fact. And I have just completed the finishing touches to the sign I have made for the door of my temporary new office:

Mr M Simpson: APT Guidance (Acting)

I can hardly believe it myself, to be honest, and I have to admit to an enormous slice of luck in the composition of the interview panel: while I fully anticipated that the views of John Ross and Richard Dick would cancel each other out, I was completely unprepared for the fact that I would be on the inside track, so to speak, with the third member of the panel as well. The lady in question was the visting PT guidance from St Ainsley's High, one of the myriad schools in which Rothesay O'Brien had been placed before her con-tinuing sojourn with us at Parkland. Mrs Welsh was frankly amazed to learn that Rothesay was still in the same school after five months, although she had – she informed me in the course of our discussion – 'heard great things' about me from Mrs O'Brien herself, who has yet another child, Raymond (from yet another marriage) at St Ainsley's.

I was a little taken aback to have her further inform me that Mrs O'Brien had credited all of Rothesay's improved attendance record to 'that pimply four-eyed lad wi' the glaikit expression' (at which revelation Mrs Welsh smiled briefly), but I chose to nod in modest – if somewhat embarrassed – agreement with the assessment.

I also have to admit to a degree of good fortune in the short-leet selection as well: to begin with, Miss Houston from Teviot Grammar had apparently mistaken Parkland High for Park*hill* High (a very different type of school altogether) in reading the job advertisement, and had failed to turn up for interview upon discovering her mistake; on the other hand, Mr Carter from Springside Secondary had apparently arrived with every intention of impressing the selection panel with his aptitude for the post. Over a friendly pre-interview coffee, however, Mr Pickup had done his best to acquaint the man with an enhanced version of some of the more inglorious incidents with which our guidance staff have had to deal over the past few years (glue-sniffing, arson attacks, assaults on staff – that kind of thing), with the understandable consequence that the man went into the interview with a decidedly ambivalent attitude to the eventual outcome.

In sharp contrast (though I say so myself), I apparently gave the impression of being a dynamic and enthusiastic go-getter who knew just what he was after – or so Richard Dick gave me to understand in my post-interview 'briefing'.

'Well done, Morris,' he shook me by the hand. 'We had a tough job persuading the boss, but it was two against one – and you're in!'

I smiled modestly and thanked him once again for all of his assistance.

'No problem,' he assured me. 'Now, can I put you down for a staff curricular development group I'm thinking of starting up for next session? Meetings twice a week, 4pm to 6pm?'

Euphoric with success, I nodded an enthusiastic agreement, for which Mr Pickup took me severely to task at our celebratory drink this evening.

'You daft bugger, Morris! Talk about Dick's pound of flesh! You're *in* now, old son: you don't *need* to keep crawling to that little fart any more.'

'Nonsense!' I contradicted him. 'Dick Dick's been very good to me this time round – and he could well do the same again, Pickup. This is just the first step on the ladder, y'know: who knows where it could end?'

'Oh my God,' he raised his eyes heavenward and started to lecture me about knowing my own limitations.

I stopped him short, thanked him for his own assistance with Mr

Carter this afternoon, and told him I wasn't going to argue with him, tonight of all nights. Whereupon I settled back to a brief, solitary reverie, Pickup's generous round – a double-measure of malt whisky – cradled warmly in my palm.

Yes, indeed – 'Morris Simpson, APT guidance'. It has a nice ring to it, I feel . . .

Friday

The last day of term, and fate has been cruel. Very cruel indeed. In what has proved to be the shortest promotion on record, I was today advised by Richard Dick to 'hold fast' on the APT guidance job.

'It should be all right, Morris, it really should be,' he tried to console me at morning break. 'It's just that the region hasn't made up its mind yet about the Rockston/Parkland merger, but it's still on the cards – and until they've decided, they've sent out a temporary hold on all new promoted posts pending a definite announcement.'

'And when will *that* be?' I wailed in frustration. 'Next week? A fortnight?'

'Couple of months, I'm afraid. New term at the earliest, more likely September.'

'September?' I wailed once again. 'September? And what am I supposed to do till then?'

'Plan for the future, Morris. Be positive. Believe you'll get the job again, even if we *do* merge.'

'And what about the sign for my office?' I almost wept in desperation. 'I spent all last night making it.'

'There, there, Morris,' Mr Dick put an arm around me. 'Stick it on the door anyway. I'm sure nobody will notice.'

Great. After seven long years, I was at last about to taste the cup of victory, only to see it dashed from my lips at very last moment.

Pickup cast me further into gloom during a consolatory drink at The Pig and Whistle after our early closure this afternoon: first of all, he announced that the hold on new posts did not, apparently, extend to Mr Ferguson's job-sharing arrangement – 'he and that bloody Froggie were still going at it hammer-and-tongs when I left the staffroom,' he informed me. Secondly, he was distressed to be the bearer of sad tidings regarding Fiona Strangelove and her announced engagement to Michael Pratt.

'No!' I gasped in astonishment. 'She can't be!'

'Well, she is.'

'But they wouldn't . . . ? They couldn't!'

'Well, I think they already *have*, actually,' he confided secretly. 'Rumour has it that this is a 'huvtie', Morris.'

'Sorry?'

'A huvtie. As in: 'ye'll huvtie get married – or else!' Understand?'

'She's not?' I replied, disbelieving at first. 'She's not . . . ? Actually . . . ? Preg . . . ?' I couldn't bring myself to say it.

''Fraid so, old son. Seven months hence for the happy event, apparently.'

I couldn't believe it. And still can't. Fiona seemed such a *nice* girl. And Michael seemed . . . ; well, Michael seemed . . .

'Yes,' cut in Pickup, apparently reading my thoughts. 'Who'd have thought he'd have had it in him, eh Simpson?'

'Who indeed, Mr Pickup?'

'Ach, to hell with them all, Morris. What d'you say to another drink, old boy?'

I accepted with understandable alacrity, as we concluded the sorry session with the toast of every teacher across the land.

'To the holidays, Mr Pickup!' I raised my glass.

'To the holidays!' he concurred. 'And long may they bloody well last!'

Postscript

It was, indeed, a cruel trick of fate that Morris Simpson's temporary promotion should prove even more temporary that he had at first envisaged. Yet this sudden reversal was perhaps no more than he should have expected: it was in line with his entire career pattern to date and – as an educationist of extraordinary optimism – he soon began to believe anew in Mr Dick's exhortations of self-belief.

And – as readers of the *Times Scottish Education Supplement* will be aware – an eventual position of somewhat dubious authority did indeed befall Simpson, once the merger debate with Rockston High had been satisfactorily resolved.

Stranger still to relate, Simpson even found it within himself to send best wishes and congratulations to Fiona Strangelove – erstwhile object of his desire – for the duration of her confinement, the full and sordid story of which pregnancy was further narrated in those subsequent diaries which were to appear in the newspaper.

At the time of writing, it is clearly too early to predict the likely level of commercial success for this, Morris Simpson's third volume of educational recollections. Should demand prove great enough, however, it is hoped that sufficient motivation – and remuneration – will be uncovered to impel Simpson towards the eventual publication of a fourth, and even a fifth collection.

But this is for the future. For the present, let us take our leave of Morris Simpson in uncertain mood, as his summer holidays begin. Like every teacher ever born, he feels he deserves them more than anybody else. And maybe he does.